CW01023489

20 Adolescent Plays and Monologues for Schools

Tackling Teen Issues and Digital Dilemmas

Gary Baxendale

First Published in 2021 by Blossom Spring Publishing
20 New World Plays and Monologues
© 2021 Gary Baxendale
ISBN 978-1-8384972-5-5
E: admin@blossomspringpublishing.com
W: www.blossomspringpublishing.com

First Published 2021
Illustrations by Diana Grebennikova.

Introduction

I have written these plays for KS3 pupils to explore challenging current global themes and issues. They focus on a changing world, changing attitudes and how smart technologies affect the lives of young children and teenagers. Children born into a digital age experience all the benefits and pitfalls of this new technology, with some, literally, left to their own 'devices'.

Each play lasts approximately 10 minutes and has been 'road tested' in my classroom ready for performance, alternatively, they can be read and studied. The 20 monologues provide 'The Given Circumstances' for each play, offering insight into the characters, context, issues and themes. Collectively, they explore close relationships: helping students to understand the importance of empathy in a world of inequality, diversity and tolerance; empowering young people to make their own changes with a hunger for hope and a brighter tomorrow.

The speaking and listening, reading and writing assignments can be used as a platform for teaching GCSE English in the National Curriculum. This resource is a working tool book for English and drama teachers, whilst also a hands-on asset to cross-curricular teaching and PHSCE in a constantly changing profession.

Gary Baxendale.

Table of Contents

.

1.   Teambuilding

Mags (Maggsey)
Jack/Jackie
Lee/Leanne
Chris/Cristine
Teacher - Sir/Miss
Paulo

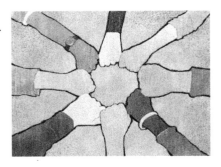

Scene: *The pupils are settling into their classroom seats, waiting for the beginning of the lesson. Lee enters later than the rest in a wheelchair.*

Mags: Oh, here he comes, watch the desks start flying. (*Whispers.*)

Chris: I heard that, Mags, you should be grateful you're not in one.

Jack: Well, you're not the one who has to move every time, just to let him through to his desk.

Mags: Yeah, shut up, Chris, or I'll knock you out of your chair.

Jack: Too right, Mags.

Chris: Tuttt, (tuts.)

Lee: Excuse me guys (*Manoeuvring the wheelchair between the desks.*)

Mags: Ahh… You've just run over my foot. (*Pretending to make a big deal of it.*)

Lee: I'm sorry, Mags, I really am, I was just getting to my desk.

Chris: There's nothing wrong with you Mags, Lee was nowhere near you.

The teacher turns to the class.

Teacher: What's going on over there?

Mags: Lee's just run over my foot, Sir.

Chris: He didn't. Sir.

Teacher: Look, is it alright or not?

Jack: Shall I take him to hospital, Sir? I think he might need an X-ray.

Mags: It's alright, Sir, I'll struggle on… with a broken foot.

Chris: As if.

Teacher: As long as you struggle on without making any more fuss. Right well, good morning class and I trust you are all well and ready for work. Ok, today we are going to be looking at what makes a successful team. So, what makes a successful team?

Chris: Working together, Sir.

Lee: Listening to each other, Sir.

Chris: Tolerance, Sir.

Teacher: Excellent, so now I'd like you to put you into groups of five to discuss and write down as many points that you can think of and why that would make a successful team.

4

Mags: Can we pick our own groups, Sir?

Teacher: No, I'm going to put the groups together, starting with you four and one more.

Mags: That means we've got to tolerate you two. *(Whispering to Chris and Lee.)*

Jack: Nice one, Mags.

Teacher: Paulo, I'd like you to join this group please, *(Sat behind the group with the teacher indicating to move.)*

Paulo: Yes, Sir *(Reluctantly and slowly.)*

Lee: Look, Chris, Paulo's coming over to join us. Let's make some room for him and make him feel comfortable.

Mags: Oh, don't tell me he's coming over to our group. I can't understand a word he says as it is.

Lee: He's just a bit shy with him being new to the school.

Chris: And in case you've already forgotten, this lesson's about team building.

Mags: Well, he's not in this team, he plays for a different one, a Spanish one I'll bet.

Jack: Yeah… too right, Mags.

Chris: You're horrible you two, give him a break.

Mags: I'd like to break you… in two.

Jack: Nice one, Mags.

5

Teacher: (*The teacher goes to where Paulo is still sat.*) Just contribute to the discussion, Paulo, the best you can, I will be circulating around the class, you'll be fine and any problems just put your hand up.

Lee: Hi Paulo, there's a seat here for you. How's things?

Paulo: Yes… I am sure what to do. (*Mags and Jack laugh at his broken response.*)

Lee: The teacher is coming back over, guys, we'd better get on with some work.

Teacher: How are we getting on over here with our list?

Chris: It's going … very slowly, Sir.

Mags: I wonder why?

Jack: Must be the team… Sir.

Teacher: Mmm, right, how can we support a team to do better? Now, that's a question and we're going to start with, Lee.

Lee: Encouragement, Sir, maybe if we support each other with our task.

Teacher: Excellent, Lee, anybody else?

Chris: To believe we can complete the challenge as a group.

Teacher: Brilliant, what do you think, Paulo?

Paulo: I not know, Sir, not sure.

Mags: He struggles with the language, Sir.

Jack: Too right, Mags.

6

Teacher: Are you two being condescending?

Mags: Not sure we understand what you mean, Sir.

Teacher: Are you patronising me? Are you two being sarcastic? *(In a firm tone)*

Mags: *(Together.)* No, Sir

Jack: *(Together.)* No, Sir.

Teacher: You better not be. *(Sternly.)* Right, ok, as a group I can see you are struggling with this verbally. So how about this, give me an example of team building physically as a group. This means you can do this practically. When I come back, shortly, I want you to show me what you have done.

Mags: Typical, now that you are in our group, the teacher is hovering around and harassing us to make sure your needs are met, and now he wants us to show our work, which we... haven't done.

Jack: Too right, it's not fair, Mags, and now we're the ones who have got to come up with something and we're the ones who are really losing out.

Mags: Because, we have to put up with you three. Lee, running over my foot, him not being able to understand even a basic task and you… for just being… annoying.

Jack: Nice one, Mags.

Chris: And don't you think everyone has had enough of you too? This is meant to be a teambuilding exercise and you've done nothing to help. All you think about is yourselves and how you can disrupt everyone and hurt their feelings. You do nothing to contribute. It's not Lee's fault he's in a wheelchair or, Paulo's, for

7

struggling with his confidence in speaking; he's new to the school and this country. Can you speak another language?

Mags: Yeah, bad language and it'll be starting soon.

Jack: Go Maggsey!

Chris: I wouldn't mind, but your own brother was badly hurt in that rugby match last year, so you know how difficult it is for Lee. You even played in the same team as him!

Mags: You leave my brother out of this.

Chris: He was always in the local paper for scoring loads of tries and you…

Mags: It's nothing to do with you, so belt up. I'm telling you.

Chris: You used to always talk about him.

Mags: Well, I don't want to talk about him now. *(Starting to raise his voice.)*

Lee: Why not?

Mags: Because he won't talk… not since… so shut it. *(Mags is shouting. There is sudden shock and silence as the rest of the class stop working and turn towards the group. Lee has his arms outstretched to Paulo who is in front of him. Paulo is walking backwards, slowly supporting Lee out of the wheelchair as he tentatively starts to walk. The class is stunned.)*

Paulo: Walk with me, I will support you. *(Lee is gently stepping out of the wheelchair.)*

Jack: Who does he think he is, the Messiah?

Mags: I thought, Lee, couldn't walk.

8

Teacher: Lee, has a degenerative muscle condition. There are very rare times, lately, when he can walk.

Chris: Let me support you also. *(The three of them are now linked together, they open their arms to Mags and Jack to join them.)* Are you part of our team?

Jack: Ha, I don't think so, do you, Mags? *(Mockingly.)*

Mags: *(There is a long pause as he eyes Jack up and down.)* Oh just...give it a rest, will you?

Jack: Looks like they're trying to make a scrum. *(Sarcastically.)*

Mags: *(Pause.)* What would you know about that, You've never played... A scrum's as strong as its weakest link... If you work as a team, you can hold it together... so it might not collapse... I just wish I'd... *(He puts his head down and slowly rises from his seat. He looks closely at the group, pauses, stands and then sincerely joins the others in the bond.)*

Jack: What ya doing, Mags? *(Jack clumsily stands up. He looks confused, awkward as he tries to join the others in the bond, It doesn't quite work for him. We see his embarrassment as he rubs his hands together nervously and sits back down in his chair.)*

~

Jack's Monologue

Characters' names can be switched on gender. Take your pick, just remember to change the pronouns.

I always thought Mags was my best friend, I've always listened to him. He's good for a laugh you see and I back him up all the time… even when I know he's wrong. I also do whatever he says… well, most of the time. So, what's with the ignoring me bit? I blame that stupid teambuilding lesson. I always thought me and Mags were the team, I just don't get it? He had a right go at me after it, saying I need to wake up. Of course, I knew his brother was in a rugby accident. He told me his brother was in a bad way and that he wouldn't even come out of his bedroom. His brother was giving up on life because of… and Mags said he couldn't accept that… and that his brother had somehow blamed him. But deep down I knew that wasn't the truth. Mags told me never to mention that to anyone, and I haven't. Now he's hanging round with Lee, pushing him in his wheelchair, holding doors open for him. He's even talking to that, Spanish kid, the one who can't string a sentence together, whilst he won't say a word… to me! I wouldn't mind, but it was, Mags, who used to show me all the posts on his Facebook page, You know… about how all these foreigners are nicking our parents' jobs. I just don't get it.

~

10

Tasks

Speaking and listening
Thinking about empathy, discuss as a group the reasons why Mags feels so bad about the past with his brother's injury. What part did he play in it? What has he learnt from the lesson on teambuilding? How has he matured as a person? **Task 1**: Improvise an imaginary scene between Mags and his brother after the teambuilding lesson. Discuss the rugby match and what might have happened. Discuss, further, the lesson and the changes in Mags because of it. This could be in a formal setting of an imaginary therapy session with a councillor who is facilitating the discussion.

Reading
After reading the dialogue and noting character differences. **Task 1:** A common trait of a play is that there is no detailed, written description of each character. You have to look for clues in what has been said in the dialogue. Now, pick any character from 'Teambuilding'. How would you describe that character from the dialogue? Note down a list of statements that lead you to imagine what they are like as a person. Next, consider their Voice, *(include accent, pitch, tone, pace.)* Gesture *(include face, body, hands, stance.)* Facial expressions (include mouth, eyes, nose, brow.) Movement (include levels, proxemics, pace, rhythm.) What makes them different from the other characters?

Writing
The play concludes with Jack questioning Mags 'What ya doing, Mags?' He is looking confused and embarrassed as he clumsily tries to join the others in the bond.

Task 1: Choose from the following options: (a) Write an essay from Jack's perspective and recollection called 'I always thought Mags was my best friend'. (b) Create an imaginary story from the past of when both boys got into trouble over an incident in or out of school and when they were best friends. (c) Write a story in the first person about what shaped you the most to make changes in your life – perhaps an experience with your family, friends, relationships, a memory, a place. or a sporting event?

Extension Task: The play is written in a naturalistic style for the actors to perform in a realistic setting. This style of acting was first introduced by Constantin Stanislavski.

Research:
https://www.bbc.co.uk/bitesize/guides/zxn4mp3/revisio
n/1. You can then complete the set tasks available online.

2. Listen

<u>Characters</u>

Characters' names can be switched on gender. Take your pick, just remember to change the pronouns.

Sarah/Saul - Teenage girl/boy
Sam/Sammy - Teenage girl/boy
Micky/Mick - Teenage girl /boy
Mrs/Mr Smith - Teacher

Scene: *Three friends are looking through the glass panel of the door to their form room.*

Sarah: Brilliant, Miss Smith's in…Watch the master at work.

Sam: I can't wait to see this.

Micky: Anything, as long as we can get out of the rain. Just don't get us into trouble… again.

They knock on the door and enter.

Sarah: Hi, Miss, are you busy?

Teacher: Yes, Sarah, I am.

Sarah: Do you want a hand with anything?

Sam: Anything at all, Miss?

Teacher: No, I'm fine thank you, girls.

Sarah: I'm so glad you're our form teacher, Miss, always there when we need you.

Teacher: And do you… need me?

Sam: No, Miss, we just thought we'd come round and see how you are.

Teacher: That's very nice of you.

Sarah: I like that jumper, Miss, very natty. You know green really suits you.

Teacher: Thank you, Sarah… What do you want? *(Sussing her out.)*

Sarah: Eh?

Micky: We just came to see if you wanted a hand with anything, Miss?

Sam: Yes, we can do anything?

Teacher: So, it's nothing to do with trying to get out of the rain?

Sarah: Ah, Miss, we'll be no trouble… honest.

Teacher: That's more than you've been for Mr Greenwood? I've just received an email from him, telling me that you and Micky have got an afterschool DT tomorrow, for talking in his lesson.

Sarah: It wasn't my fault, Miss, I was only talking about the lesson! *(Micky is in disbelief.)*

Teacher: Really?

Micky: Would you like us to tidy your bookcase up for you, Miss, we'll do a really good job if you give us a chance?

Sarah: Yes, Miss, we can get it all organised for you, and those shelves!

14

Teacher: Can I trust you to do that? I've got a lot of marking to do and I still have to prepare for my next lesson?

Sam: Miss, we'll be as good as…

Teacher: OK girls, you can come in and do the shelves, but don't let me down, I'm trusting you.

All: We won't.

The girls start to tidy up the shelves quietly all smiling at each other and Mrs Smith.

Teacher: Girls, I just have to pop out to get these sheets photocopied. Remember what I said, please.

All: Yes, Miss
She exits and the girls sit down.

Sarah: What am I..? Genius, that's what!

Micky: I think it was more of a team effort, actually.

Sam: Sarah did most of the talking though, Micky.

Micky: We know that! It's Sarah's talking that got us kicked out of the canteen.

Sarah: That is so unfair.

Sam: Actually, it was because your phone started to ring.

Micky: Loudly… and you even answered it!

Sarah: That is such a stupid rule anyway, and now they've confiscated it.

Sam: I agree, Sarah, it's so wrong.

Micky: Well, we all got kicked out of the canteen for it.

Sam: Emm, that's true, and I was really enjoying that apple and custard pie.

Micky: Come on, let's get on with this tidying up?

Sarah: You can get on with it, there's not enough work for three of us.

Sarah sits down away from the girls as they work on the bookcase and shelves.

Sam: What's that noise?

Sarah: It's probably some, loser, playing outside in the rain.

Sam: There it is again. It's coming from that window. Look, there's a cat, stranded on the ledge outside!

Sarah: No way, how did it get there?

Sam: Poor thing, it looks terrified!

Sarah: We've got to get it inside. Hey, Mickey, come look at this, there's a cat stuck just outside the window.

Mickey: Let's have a look, don't go near it, Sarah, it might jump. It looks like it hasn't eaten in weeks. I'm going to get, Miss.

Mickey leaves.

Sarah: No need for any of that hassle, I'll sort this out now.

Sam: Don't, Sarah! If it jumps off it'll die, just wait for a teacher.

Mickey returns with Mrs Smith.

Mrs Smith: What's this about a cat stuck on a ledge? I hope for your sake you're not having me on, Mickey.

Sam: No, Miss, she isn't, come look. It even has a collar on, it's someone's pet. I wonder why it came up here.

Mrs Smith: Sam, it's an animal. It doesn't understand the consequences of its actions. Right, the best thing to do is to get a caretaker to place a safety net underneath this window, then if worse comes to worst and it jumps, it should be ok. I'll be back with a caretaker in a minute. Whatever you do, don't go near that cat.

Mrs Smith leaves.

Sarah: I hate cats me. I don't understand what the big fuss is about.

Mickey: Even if you don't like cats, this is still someone's pet. The owner must be worried sick.

Sarah: Oh, put a sock in it ya big baby. This has gone on for too long, I'll fix this in two seconds.

Sam: Don't go near the window, Sarah, please.

Sarah: And you too now?

Mickey: Mrs Smith, told us not to approach the cat, if she hears that you disobeyed her, you'll be in detention for months.

Sarah: You'll be singing my praises soon!

Sarah moves towards the cat. It jumps from the ledge. Outside, Mrs Smith

17

sees the cat fall as she turns the corner with a caretaker. She shouts up to the students.

Mrs Smith: Who went near that cat?

Sarah: No one, Miss, it just jumped for no reason.

Mrs Smith: No reason? I'll be up in one minute; you'd better get your stories straight.

Mickey: You are in so much trouble.

Sarah: You've got to cover for me. Mickey... Sam..?

~

Mickey's Monologue

Micky is outside the Heads office, waiting to be reprimanded.

Sarah's been in there ages now. The head sounds furious. The shouting is making me feel worse. I bet Sarah gets suspended and then… I'm in next, I think I need the toilet. My mum will go absolutely spare when she finds out what's happened. First the DT with Mr Greenwood…. Sarah's fault, then, sent out of the dining room at lunchtime… Sarah's fault. And finally, that poor cat… Sarah… again. *(She starts to get upset.)* I can still hear the bell on its collar and still see its poor face, it was terrified. Its owners have been notified and they're coming up to school. They want some answers... and that means, I'll have to tell the truth, that it was Sarah's fault… And if I drop her in it, that would be the end of our friendship, she'll never speak to me again… ever! But would she drop me in it? Oh no, the head's office door is opening, I'm next…

~

Tasks

Speaking and listening
This activity is to encourage the students to think about the reasons the three characters get into trouble. **Task 1:** In-class discussion, what makes the characters different from one another? Create a list giving at least 5 examples of their speech and actions in the play. **Task 2:** Each student is to think about the person they are sat next to in class. Discuss the differences and similarities between each other. Try to find at least 3 of each. **Task 3:** Back to the script: Discuss, in pairs, how you could create another scene. This could be from the past or in the future, where one of the characters gets the other into trouble and blames their friend/peer, rather than being honest and owning up to the mistake they have made. This could be in or out of school. Alternatively, this could be improvised and then performed to the group in class.

Reading
Looking back through the script, what evidence is there that Sarah is going to get the others into trouble? **Task 1:** Consider the ways that people manipulate other people and make a list of devices that could be used to avoid getting into these situations. For example, anticipating what could happen next and how could you change it? **Task 2:** What would you classify as good behaviour in school? How would that benefit your learning in school, in life after school and your work and prosperity in the future? Create a poster on what you feel is acceptable behaviour and how this would be a benefit to all students.

Writing
The play leaves the students in serious trouble. Imagine the owner of the cat has contacted a local newspaper who then published a story about it.

20

Task 1: Research newspaper headlines in your local paper, look at the way the stories are constructed, e.g., subtitles, paragraph structures and content. This can be done through old copies of local papers or an online activity. **Task 2:** Create the article, with a headline, story and interviews with the cat owner and the head of the school. Remember these key points: What happened? Where did this happen? Who was involved? Why did it happen?

Extension Task: Writing about important events is a useful skill to learn. Check out how to write a news article:
https://www.bbc.co.uk/bitesize/topics/zgqxwnb/articles/zbsbwty

2. No One To Talk To

Characters
Maddie
Terri
Lucy
Debs

Maddie: *(Speaking in a 'direct address' to the audience.)* I met Terri, on the first day at High School. We were just like a couple of goldfish, swimming alone in this really big deep pond. I met up with her by accident. We were sat next to each other in registration. I didn't have a choice really, the teacher made that for us. My surname's, Addison and Terri's is, Baker. Terri, used to carry all her equipment around in a plastic bag, it had an expensive 'Logo' on it, but I don't think she'd ever shopped there. We didn't see much of each other between lessons until.

Scene: *Break time and Terri is silently crying outside on her own.*

Maddie: Hiya, are you ok?

Terri: Not really.

Maddie: Why what's happened?

Terri: Miss, shouted at me.

Maddie: What for?

Terri: I didn't have a pen.

Maddie: You can have one of mine, I don't mind.

22

Enter Lucy and Debs.

Lucy: What's going on?

Maddie: I think it's sorted.

Debs: No need to cry then, is there?

Lucy: We're, Lucy and Debs, Hi ya, we're not in any of your classes?

Maddie: No, I thought I hadn't seen you. I'm, Maddie and this is…Terri.

Lucy pulls out her phone without being seen by any teachers.

Lucy: Shall we friend each other?

Debs: Yeah, we've got the biggest group in our year.

Maddie: Er, okay, *(Reluctantly pulling out her phone.)*

Debs: And you?

Terri: I don't have a phone.

Lucy and Debs: What?

Lucy: Where you been for the last 5 years?

Debs: Mars?

Maddie: *(Direct address.)* Terri, didn't have a phone, Terri, didn't have anything. Her uniform was her charity shop best, mixed together with the school uniform. Throughout Year 7, both were looking worse for wear and shorter by the day. The teachers were always going on about it. In PE I used to bring a spare kit for,

23

Terri, it was always the same,

In the girls dressing room.

Terri: Maddie, can I borrow your shorts again, please? Mrs Roberts will go spare with me, I've forgotten my kit again.

Maddie: Of course you can, but what are you going to run in?

Terri: I'm going to run in my trainers, I'll take my socks off so they don't get wet, I can put them on after we get back.

Lucy and Debs are eavesdropping.

Lucy: Err, your feet will stink!

Debs: Yeah, I wondered where that horrible smell was coming from.

Lucy: And don't bother trying to borrow a top from me again, I still haven't got it back, not that I'd want it, now.

Debs: Not that you would, Luce, it'd be infested with nits.

Lucy: Probably walks on its own now, over to her best mate, Maddie.

Debs: Yeah, a right pair of nits! Haaaa.

Maddie:*(Direct address.)* We didn't answer them back, it was just best to keep out of their way, as did most of our year group. In the summer holidays, Terri, came to our house to play, sometimes after school or at the weekends. My dad used to ask, 'Why can't you go to, Terri's house, once in a while?' I'm pretty sure he knew why, I mean, my dad is not unkind, it's just he must have felt, he'd adopted her. She was always at our house. She just said, her mum was always busy with her new boyfriend, I knew better than to

24

push it with her any further, mainly, as boyfriend issues were all I heard about at school in Year 8.

Debs and Lucy shielding their phones from the eyes of any teacher.

Debs: So, what did he say, Luce? Come on, don't keep us in suspense.

Lucy: He said, 'I think I like you.'

Debs: I knew it, I knew it, you can tell. What you gonna text back to him?

Lucy: Watch this… 'I think I like U 2.'

Debs: Go, girl… Eh, Luce, look over there, Tatty Terri's got a phone. I don't believe it.

Lucy: Where did that, flea bag get the money from? Let's check who she's texting. *(They walk over to Terri.)*

Debs: See you've got a phone, at last.

Lucy: What's it run on… steam?

Debs: *(snatches it.)* Look, Luce, it's so old, it's got hieroglyphics on the back of it.

Lucy: Oh, don't be rotten, Debs, at least it's got a screen, even if it is cracked.

Terri: Give it back to me, I need it.

Debs: Oh, are you contacting your, boyfriend then?

Lucy: Yeah, I'll bet she has a long list to choose from.

25

Terri: I was just messaging my friend.

Lucy: Well, we're your, friends, aren't we, Debs?

Debs: Unless, we're not good enough for you?

Lucy: So… let's friend each other.

Terri: Yes, but…

Debs: Come on then… *(The phone pings the notification.)*

Lucy and Debs: Thank you… Muppet.

Maddie: *(Direct address.)* I might have told her not to do it, but I was keeping my distance from Terri towards the end of Year 8. She seemed to attract more of the attention of, Lucy and Debs. To be honest, I was scared for her but mainly for myself. The pair of them were horrible, constantly bragging about their boyfriends in the year above. When I thought things couldn't get any worse for, Terri… they did.

Lucy: I think 'Tatty' needs a boyfriend, Debs?

Debs: Yeah, why should we be so selfish Luce, and take them all.

Lucy: That's why we're so generous, Debs, to our good friend 'Tatty'. Say 'Cheese'

Debs quickly takes a photo of the shocked Terri.

Terri: What you doing? You can't do that.

Debs: We, just have darling.

Terri: What you gonna do with it?

26

Lucy: We're gonna create a page for ya, and help you find a boyfriend.

Debs: Yeah, it's gonna have your mugshot on it.

Lucy: 'Boyfriend wanted, dead or alive?' It won't take you long... to find the profile.

Maddie: *(Direct address.)* Unfortunately, neither did anyone else. It was written on the girl's toilet wall. Everyone was talking about it. I didn't talk to her and I avoided eye contact with, Terri, throughout this time. I was too embarrassed. I smiled, when someone showed it to me on the wall... but deep down, my stomach was rolling. When our Head of Year found out about it, she went ballistic with Lucy and Debs...They were nearly expelled. In the canteen on Tuesday lunchtime, I was sat down at the table, Terri walked past me. I kept my head down, when I lifted it up, she was sat opposite me.

Terri: Hi, Maddie, I've been hoping to catch up.

Maddie: Err, yeah, Err, what for?

Terri: Just, to talk with you.

Maddie: Oh, err, right.

Terri: You, seem to be avoiding me... throughout this past year.

Maddie: I'm not... I'm just busy you know.

Terri: I thought we were, friends, or at least we used to be?

Maddie: I am, Terri... but people change you know.

Terri: I know.

Maddie: Well, er… I guess I should be…

Terri: I've made some new friends now, Maddie.

Maddie: Good, how… I mean where?

Terri: Online.

Maddie: Really?

Terri: And, I just have to tell you something, that I've met someone really nice.

Maddie: Yeah?

Terri: I mean, really nice… I think I'm in love with him.

Maddie: You've met a boyfriend online?

Terri: I can talk to him about anything, we message each other every night.

Maddie: What do you 'message' him about then?

Terri: You know… him… me, … his family, my family, well, not much about my family, but you know… Do you want to see a picture of him, he's gorgeous?

Maddie: *(Startled.)* Sure, What's his name anyway?

Terri: *(She discreetly shows a picture of him on her phone.)* Danny, I'm meeting him in town this Saturday afternoon, outside the cinema. I can't believe it, he's soooo nice.

Maddie: He looks really nice… but are you sure about this, I mean, are you sure it's him?

28

Terri: I'm not stupid you know; I know all about the weirdos and the dangers of online friends. That's why I'm asking a big favour from you.

Maddie: What?

Terri: I can't ask my mum, not that she'd come anyway… but if you could come with me, just to check him out, you know, so to speak, make sure everything's… alright?

Maddie: Well, I've got plans for, er… Saturday.

Terri: Oh, come on, Maddie, just this once… Please say…Yes?

Maddie: Well, I, er, alright… Yes.

Terri: Oh, thanks, Maddie, I won't forget this.

Maddie: *(Direct address.)* I did it partly out of guilt for letting, Terri, down in the past, partly out of protecting her, because she would be on her own out there, but mainly out of curiosity to see what, Danny, was actually like. I mean he did look a bit hot. Was I jealous, I'm not sure? Saturday came and we met up as agreed, Danny was late!

Terri: Thanks for coming, Maddie, do I look Ok?

Maddie: You look… great, Terri.

Terri: But he's late, do you think he's seen me and ran off?

Maddie: No… just give him time, he might have missed his bus… anything could have happened.

Maddie: Just then, a van drove past us tooting its horn. We heard someone shout, 'Terri' and a hand was waving us over. They were having trouble pulling over, because of the traffic.

29

Terri: It's him, his father's dropping him off. Stay here a sec, I'll go and check. Do I look Ok?

Maddie: Yes, Terri, you look great. Don't run, you'll look too keen. I'll wait here for you.

Maddie: And, then she walked over to the van, clutching her bag excitedly, trying to stop herself from breaking into a fast step. But something was wrong, she spoke to his father in the van and came running back to me.

Terri: Oh no, Maddie, Danny's broke his leg playing football this morning. He's in hospital, it's fractured in 5 places. His father said he keeps asking about me, he's going to take me there now. Thanks, Maddie, I owe you one.

Maddie: Terri, wait a minute, please… *(She stops, turns and speaks to the audience.)*
And then she was off… to the hospital.
But she never got there… did she Officer?

~

Terri's Monologue

Terri is preparing her dinner in the kitchen.

There's not much in the fridge, just these frozen fish fingers, they'll do, they'll have to do. I hope putting the oven on, doesn't cut the electricity off like it did last night. By the time we got it sorted, it was late in the evening and my dinner was ruined. I don't complain though, well not to mum, she's got enough on her plate… and I don't mean food. I want to tell my mum, about what's happening at school with Lucy and Debs, but I can't. It's because I know she's got her own problems… and I'm well, really worried about her. What's bothering her? I know, something's on her mind, but she won't tell me. It's like she's, just staring into space. I try talk to her and she tells me she 'loves me' and I tell her 'I love her too.' She seems to be waiting for her boyfriend to return her messages but he seems just another 'Waster.' When I get older, I'm gonna make sure no boyfriend messes me around. That's why, Danny, is so perfect. He always answers my texts, says lovely things about me and really understands me. When I think about him, I get butterflies in my stomach, like it's in knots. Oh, he's so good looking. I just can't wait to meet him in person, instead of texting. It's like playing phone tennis. *(Her phone pings.)* Oh, I don't believe it, he wants to meet this Saturday afternoon outside the cinema. *(She pulls her arms in towards her stomach, looks up excitedly and sighs.)*

~

Tasks

Speaking and listening
In the play, 'No One To Talk To' Terri appears difficult to communicate with and is very insecure. How could you help to put someone at ease? **Task 1**: In pairs, discuss how you can help to put someone at ease through conversation. What advice would you give? **Task 2:** Now, in pairs, practice asking a question with a question. For example, in pairs
A: What did you do over the weekend?
B: I went into town, I was looking for a case for my phone… What did you do?
A: I went to the park, but it started raining… did you get a case for your phone?
B: Yes, I got one on the market, it's Ok … What did you do when it started raining?

Now try and continue the conversation through improvising. How does this help keep the conversation going by answering a question with a question? **Task 3:** Maddie, acts as the narrator at various points throughout the play. Now in your group, create a narrated mime, with each actor making clear expressions and gestures to the audience whilst she is narrating. This can be made clearer and highlighted by the vocals of Maddie, recounting the various parts of the story in a scared, happy, nervous, excited voice.

Reading
Looking again at the characters in the play: Create a drawing of a human figure on a sheet of paper, this can be as basic as a 'Gingerbread' figure to do this task.
Write 'Role on the Wall' above the figure and the name of the chosen character. This is a technique developed by the practitioner Constantin Stanislavski. It is where the actor writes down as much information they have collated about the character. This is in the form of an outline of a male/female. The 'Given circumstances' are the clues revealed through the words and

32

actions of the character in the play. **Task 1:** Pick a character from the play and on the outside of the shape, write down all the facts you know about your chosen character, e.g., name, age, class, family, relationship with other characters. On the inside of the shape, write down other information- some of which you can make up, using your imagination. I.e., What type of personality they have, how they dress, look, behave, characteristics, such as are they shy, nervous?

Writing
A monologue is a speech that expresses the thoughts and feelings of a character in a play. It is quite similar to a diary extract without the 'Dear Diary' beginning. *(Look at Terri's, monologue as an example.)*
Task 1: Carrying on from the 'Role on the Wall' exercise, write a monologue for your chosen character from the play. Try and use your imagination, to add new information, that isn't revealed in the play to create a further background to your character. Alternatively, pick a particular point in time from the beginning, middle or the end of the play.

Extension Task: The best way to present your monologue is through performance. Take a look at:
https://www.youtube.com/watch?v=C2NQSP25tUo
Through the examples shown of performing monologues, practice yours ready for class.

4. Facing the Truth

Characters
Jagdeep
Frankie

Characters' names can be switched on gender. Take your pick, just remember to change the pronouns.
Jag and Frankie are walking home from school together.

Jag: What did you think of that last lesson, Frankie?

Frankie: Alright… why?

Jag: Healthy relationships… thought that would be right up your street with all your admirers?

Frankie: The bit about 'romantic competence' was right up my street, the part about homework is the pits. I mean, look at this worksheet,… give me a break. I've got swimming practice tonight… and now this! *(He pulls out the sheet and passes it to, Jagdeep.)*

Jag: Give two examples of respect, security and communication in a friendship?

Frankie: Give me a break, I'd switched off long before then. It was only the 'intimacy' bit that woke me up.

Jag: Ah… I thought that would be the part when you moved your head off the table, but I think the teacher was talking about this: *(He points to a part in the worksheet.)* preparations for 'romantic competence' with… future relationships.

Frankie: Hey, I'm on it, I'm totally prepared.

34

Jag: So, you think you're ready for a relationship?

Frankie: Jag... I was born ready; you should know that. Girls, are like a magnet to me, I even had a following in Year 5.

Jag: Yeah… but how do you know what you want, what you need… now?

They stop walking.

Frankie: Simple, they'll be attractive to look at... say no more, end of story, we all live happily ever after.

Jag: Yeah, but what if like, you get bored of their attractive… 'Looks'… and they get bored of you, maybe you've got nothing interesting to say to each other? Then you start arguing, falling out, you know, that contempt thing the teacher was on about?

Frankie: Are you telling me that a girl could get bored of me, or I could pick the wrong one? Get real, I could have the choice of any girl in our year!

Jag: Maybe, but even you could get it wrong… I think the lesson was mainly about lasting friendships… developing skills to have a healthy friendship, not just physically but mentally.

Frankie: Heav…y Jag… You must have been the only one listening in class, I was more interested in the physical parts of it!

Jag: I'll bet you were, … But I was thinking about this, *(He raises the worksheet.)* The 'insight' part of the lesson, remember that? So, you can both learn from mistakes.

Frankie: Why, have you made some?

Jag: Not sure, yet.

Frankie: How do you mean?

Jag: It's, just difficult.

Frankie: What are you on about?

Jag: Well, you know about compromising… when someone makes a mistake or says something out of turn.

Frankie: Well, I_could compromise, even in a relationship… providing they apologised first.

Jag: But, part of the homework is about 'mutuality' It asks, *(He shows him the sheet.}* How you could communicate your feelings openly, to support both of your needs?

Frankie: Alright then, I'd apologise too, how's that sound…? But not… and I mean not, if I'm kept waiting, I hate that, you know waiting, when someone doesn't reply to you. Like you've sent a text and you're left waiting for an answer.

Jag: *(Jagdeep pulls out his phone and stares at it.)* But, anything could have happened, the phone might have gone flat, they might not have got the message, anything. Sometimes, you've got to be patient… or not respond too quickly, you know, give it time to think about?

Frankie: Listen, I'm the most patient guy there is… but I hate being messed about.

Jag: But, could you keep calm, offer support… to a friend?

Frankie: To you, Jag, anything. We're solid. *(Frankie, holds Jag in a grip and kisses his forehead.)*

Jag: You really believe that, Frankie? *(Jagdeep smiles and starts typing on his phone.)*

36

Frankie: I'm a rock to my mates. *(He starts singing 'Never gonna give you up' in a sarcastic manner and puts his arm around, Jagdeep.)* Never gonna give you up, never gonna let you down. *(Jag, accidentally pushes the send button on the text he's been writing.)*

Jag: Oh, shhh…

Frankie: What's up? *(His phone pings… takes it out of his pocket and reads the text.)* 'I think I luv U x.'… What, Who's this to...?

Jag: I'm, sorry, Frankie… I didn't mean to send that.

Frankie: Oh yeah, you been keeping that quiet. Who's the lucky girl then?

Jag: Well… er, the compromise bit we were talking about earlier…

Frankie: Yeah?

Jag: And the offering support bit…

Frankie: Yeah?

Jag: Well… it's er… sent to you, Frankie'

Frankie: What? … You can't be serious, Jag?

Jag: I'm, totally serious, mate, I really am and I know, I'm taking a big risk.

Frankie: You're telling me you are! What…what you doing this for?

Jag: I just want you to listen to me,

Frankie: Listen… are you for real ..? I've gotta go.

37

Jag: No, hold on, Frankie. Let me explain.

Frankie: No, you hold on, this is freaking me out. I've got to go.

Jag: I'm sorry, Frankie… will you keep it to yourself?

Frankie: *(Stunned.)* Yeah, yeah, sure, I won't breathe a word. *(He walks away.)*

A week later, Frankie is nervously looking around as Jagdeep approaches.

Jag: Why did you do it?

Frankie: Do what?

Jag: You know, don't give me that…

Frankie: Give you what?

Jag: You know what… that 'I don't know what you're on about look.'

Frankie: It's the truth, I don't know what you're on about.

Jag: Well, you're the only person I've mentioned it to… and now everybody knows.

Frankie: Don't look at me, it's not my fault.

Jag: Yes, it is… You promised me and I trusted you.

Frankie: Well, you shouldn't have sent me that text, telling me… you're gay.

Jag: No, I didn't say that. I said… I luv… but I'm not sure.

Frankie: And, are you… gay?

38

Jag: That's not the point, the point is… you promised me, you said 'I won't breathe a word.'

Frankie: Well, I wasn't exactly expecting that, I mean we've known each other all these years... And now I mean…

Jag: Don't flatter yourself. You know after the conversation we were having, at the very least, you'd show me some respect and keep it private.

Frankie: I have.

Jag: Well, how come everybody knows and is talking about it, saying things behind my back. Do you know how hard that is for me, who can I now turn to for support?

Frankie: Well, I wasn't exactly happy either.

Jag: So… did tell your parents?

Silence.

Jag: And then, you told people in our form.

Frankie: No... well… only Janet.

Jag: And Janet told Chris, and Chris told Richard, who then told others and now…. everyone knows. Do you remember our conversation… healthy relationships... and what about that other thing … romantic ..?'

Frankie: … Competence.

Jag: Incompetence ..! And now you've made it even harder for me… by going viral.

Frankie: Yeah, I've er... seen it.

39

Jag: Everyone knows, Frankie, some are spreading homophobic comments about me.

Frankie: That's not my fault.

Jag: Well, who's fault is it?

Silence.

Jag: You know, the worst part was getting changed in PE, everybody looking at me, pretending that I'm looking at them. Making sly comments to each other, you know, you've heard them, and done... absolutely, nothing. Do you know how awkward that feels, Frankie?

Frankie: Look I'm sorry, Jags, I er really didn't think it would get like this... But what can I do about it?

Jag: Standing by me would be a start.

Frankie: I don't know if I can do that, I mean...

Jag: You're scared of what others might think of you, being associated with me.

Frankie: I'm afraid of no one… I er... I don't know. I mean, what can I do… or you do?

Jag: Well, I know what I'm going to do, I've made up my mind. I've spoken to, Miss Wieclawski and we are going to start an LGBT club in school,

Frankie: Miss Wieclawski, I didn't know she was gay?

Jag: I don't think she is, but who cares. She just wants to change these outdated attitudes from some of the kids in this school.

40

Frankie: *(Rolling eyes.)* Yeah, alright… I get it.

Jag: So, an LGBT club in school. 'Life Gets Better Today.'

Frankie: So, are you gonna… 'Come out' like?

Jag: I've been living in conflict for so long, and now… I've had enough of this nonsense… you just watch me, stand and watch if you like. Do nothing for all I care because… I can accept who I am.

Frankie: So… Who are you? What are you?

Jag: I'm me, and I'm going to learn to love people, the people I do love.

Frankie: That's gonna be some call, you know how some of them are… when they know you are… you know.

Jag: Gay.

Frankie: But what if people can't accept you for that?

Jag: Then, they'll just have to get over it. Maybe, I'll have some people that will stand by me… 'I'm like a rock to my mates.' Do you remember that? Or maybe not.

Frankie: You're a tough nut, Jag, do you know that?

Jag: Believe it, Frankie, I am.

Frankie: More than I ever thought possible, Jagdeep. *(Frankie, has his head down, smiles to himself and looks Jagdeep in the eyes.)*… I can't promise anything, but I'll try, Jags… I really am sorry; of all the friends I've had… got. I never wanted to hurt you. It just seemed such a big thing at the time, but now… who cares what they think…*(He puts his arm around, Jagdeep and holds him close.)* I'm so sorry

41

for letting you down...You're my best friend. *(An imaginary pupil is watching this moment as Frankie looks over Jag's shoulder and shouts.)* Oi... What's your problem?

~

Frankie's Monologue

Characters' names can be switched on gender. Take your pick, just remember to change the pronouns.

The first time I stood on the top board and walked to the edge, I looked down at the water and my stomach rolled. I could see the bottom of the pool, it looked so far down. It was the first time in my life I felt really frightened and I stepped back. When I saw the comments on my phone, I felt… you know that same feeling… that feeling in your stomach, like it's turning and it makes you feel sick and it's not because I'm stood on the top board or I've eaten anything bad. It's just that I know, I've done something wrong. Is that your conscience? I don't know, nobody's explained to me, no one's needed to… till now. Is it regret, shame, anger, the feeling of letting a friend down? To cap it all, I had PE last lesson… 'Oh, I hate Badminton, It's sooo GAY'… Richard's, sly remark, setting the others off in fits of giggles, rolling their eyes on, Jagdeep and then turning to me… for my reaction... all eyes were on me, waiting for me to laugh, or smile with them, join together with them. Be one of them… against my friend. I looked and… I didn't laugh… but… I smiled back… and there it was, my shame. I'd betrayed, my best friend, who I've known since... I keep getting this wave…. Of knowing that I've done something wrong… but is it my fault? NO… It's Jagdeep's fault. Why, would he come out with such a thing like that? He's made things so bad for himself, why, couldn't he just keep quiet about his…feelings, thoughts, changes, whatever? I'm gonna keep out of his way for a while, that's his problem. *(He puts his head down and then looks up.)* … isn't it?

~

Tasks

Speaking and listening

Accepting who we are is key to individuality, celebrating our differences and our similarities are key to a fair society. Look at extracts of the speech 'More Winners' written by Donna Okonjo. What are the main points she is making? How does she make an impact on her audience? **Task 1:** Write a small speech that you could prepare for your class or school assembly on 'Acceptance of who you are and what you want to be when you are older, considering your moral values.' **Task 2:** Now it is written, practice delivering your speech, focusing on what you want to say to your audience, all the time imagining, you are in front of a TV camera. Try to make it passionate and show that it is something you fully believe in to get their fullest attention.

'More Winners" – Donna Okonjo

How many times do we ask the same question Why is inequality all around us? We are told to compete, but with so little space left on the podium, it leaves no place for the rest of the field. They are left to watch from the sidelines. The bigger question is, how do we make the podium big enough for more of us to fit on? The differences surrounding us, ineffective policies, are suffocating not only our fullest potential but our last breath. This has, literally, been under a knee on the street or the iron heel of stagnation. Instead of embracing the diversity around us, the focus has been on the differences between us. Surely, if we focus on our similarities, that can be the glue that can hold us together.

With many underprivileged children dropping out of education, they are losing sight, direction and hope. But every dream matters and we need a vision that gives young people direction. Dreams can become a reality through resilience, empowerment and motivation. Out of that, comes higher earnings, coupled with lower mortalities.

When more people benefit from countries' rising GDPs and boosted disposable incomes, the feeling of belonging to society embraces the individual, family and country. But firstly, we must learn to love ourselves, to have our own, personal respect. Then, and only then, can we protect, respect and care for one another.

44

In life, there are winners and losers, but we can train the builders to construct a larger podium, we can train the teachers to give society's disadvantaged a more equal footing to get on the podium. And finally, when we become part of that team, more can share in the fruits of that success, and that surely is a winning team.

Reading

A dramatic pause is a short or long silence *(a moment of stillness in the action to make the audience think)* used in drama to create tension and atmosphere in a certain part of the scene. **Task 1**: Make a list of dramatic pauses used in the play to add more tension. Alternatively, look at the play and make a list of keywords that you could emphasise *(this is called intonation in the voice)* to make a stronger point of view.

Writing

Teachers have a duty of care in promoting the safety, health and welfare of children under their supervision. A school report by 'Stonewall' concluded that nearly half (45%) of LGBT, pupils are bullied in school. How can we change or influence the conversations we have with our friends and family about homophobia into something more helpful for LGBT students? **Task 1**: Write two contrasting stories **or** scenes for a play about a teenager 'coming out' to their parents. One, a fantasy of how they would want it to turn out, in contrast to the actual reality in the other scene. Which one would you want to perform first? Consider this before you start writing.

Extension Task: Research motivational speeches on how to inspire people to change their viewpoints and understanding of life. Look at Denzel Washington's speech on Dreaming Big. https://www.youtube.com/watch?v=_9BcM2de4gE

5. Lost In Spaces

Physical Theatre *is using your body to create shapes, objects, props and letters. It is used frequently in modern theatre because it is inexpensive, and the actor and the audience have to use more imagination to engage with the performance.*

<u>Characters</u>
Actor 1 – Captain Lyndon Price
Actor 2 – First Officer Lee
Actor 3 – Navigator Sanchez
Actor 4 – Communications Officer Imani
Actor 5 – Commodore

Scene: *The bridge of the 'Starship of Freedom.'*

Lee: 'What piece of work is a man. How noble in reason, how infinite in faculty. In form and moving, how express and admirable. In action how like an angel, in apprehension how like a god! The beauty of the world. The paragon of animals. And yet…'

Actors 2, 3, 4 & 5 <u>*Create the Captain's chair and consul with levers, pads and dials.*</u>

Captain: Captain Lyndon Price, flight recording 7529 of the ships daily log. Mission statement… to spread goodwill and prosperity to all lifeforce we encounter. The crew have all been picked for their expertise, individuality and obedience. They know this ship is on a dangerous mission and some will be lost along the way. But they have a captain they believe in, you could say… the best in the fleet. Ask anyone on board this tremendously beautiful and utterly unique 'Starship of Freedom'.

Actors 2, 3, 4 & 5 <u>*Create the 'The Starship of Freedom' Then altogether come out onto the imaginary bridge to say the lines in unison.*</u>

All Actors: We come in peace.

Imani: Message coming in from Earth, Captain,

Captain: Put it on the screen, Imani.

Actors 2, 3, & 4 _Create the 'Screen' for the Commodore._

Commodore: Captain Price, this message is of the utmost importance. It is the top priority.

Captain: Yes, Commodore, relay your orders.

Commodore: We want you to go on a diplomatic mission to, Icarus 5.

Sanchez: Captain, we are just approaching that sector.

Captain: Lucky for us, Navigator Sanchez.

Commodore: Your orders are to go there at once and make contact with the species of that planet. Our previous scanning of the planet detects large reserves of Marzipluto and I'm sure you know only too well what that means to us. Our communication devices run on it and we have big shortages, so… diplomacy is the word… Get that Marzipluto!

Captain: Gotcha, Commodore. No one knows diplomacy better than I do. We are shortly entering their solar system..? They'll be no threat. Over.

Commodore: I'll leave it in your capable hands, Captain… Over.

Captain: Huh, We certainly can't allow other planets to stop our progress. Navigator Sanchez, lay on a course for Icarus 5.

Actors 2, 3 and 4 *come out of the screen to create the imaginary bridge of the 'Starship'.*

Sanchez: Already plotted and laid in, Captain. Do you want me to deploy weapons?

Captain: Good thinking, Sanchez… but not yet… Imani, contact Icarus 5 and tell them to be expecting us.

Imani: Yes, Captain.

Captain: First Officer, what do we know about these, Icarunian's?

Lee: To our knowledge, an isolated peaceful nation, half-bird, half-reptile in nature. Certainly non-aggressive.

Captain: Ok, Imani, patch me through to the higher council. (*Imani does so.*) This is, Captain Lyndon Price of the 'Starship of Freedom.' We come in peace, in fact, we are the most peaceful race in the universe. That's not just me saying that; it's also other planetary leaders. They say we're beautifully peaceful and… No one has come close, ask anyone..? We would like to trade with you, for your, Marzipluto, and give you a unique deal, to give you wealth, tremendous wealth. It'll be perfect, beautifully wealthy perfect. What do you say?

Actors 2, 3, 4 & 5 Multi *Rolling and creating the 'Icarunian of half-bird – half-reptile. It speaks in turn.*

Actor 2: *We do not crave wealth.*

Actor 3: *You are a warlike species and primitive.*

Actor 4: *We know of your history.*

Actor 5: *You are barbaric with savage intent.*

48

Actor 2: *Leave us in our own peace.*

Actor 3: There will be no shipments of, Marzipluto.

Actor 4: Do not attempt to land on the planet surface.

Actor 5: This is not a request.

Captain: Someone has been spreading fake news about us. Don't you know this is the 'Starship of Freedom?' In the spectrum of weapons, we have unbelievable firepower that could… obliterate the entire galaxy. Just ask any of our adversaries, there's nothing left of them… but… we come in peace.

Actors 2, 3, 4 & 5: *(Speaks as one)* Just leave us in peace!

Captain: Isn't that typical. I knew this would happen, Sanchez, I've decided you're coming with me.

Actors 2, 3, 4 & 5 *Revert to characters on the 'Starship of Freedom.*

Sanchez: You bet, Captain.

Imani: Err… they do have a good point, Captain, they just want to be left alone.

Captain: Nonsense. Look at the deal they'll get.

Imani: They're not interested in deals, Captain.

Captain: Tell them… we'll remove their air.

Lee: They don't breathe air, Captain, they live in the water.

Captain: Just part of a negotiating strategy. Ok, we'll remove the water then.

49

Lee: Vaporise the water?

Sanchez: We can bomb them, Captain.

Captain: Good point again, Sanchez, maybe negotiating makes us look weak. Right, I'll pass on the transporter, I don't fancy materialising in the water when I'm talking to those flying turtles. We're taking the shuttle instead, plus it's got more firepower.

Imani: No… that is so wrong. They're a peaceful species.

Lee: Captain, I do concur with Officer Imani, they show no hostile intent.

Captain: No one could have come close to predicting this response from those Guppies, but fortunately I've been bestowed with unbelievable intuition. I had a gut response about this all along. Are we fully armed, Sanchez?

Sanchez: Ready, Captain, locked and loaded.

Captain: First Officer Lee, I leave you in charge of the ship, we're heading down there.

Sanchez: Officer Lee, where is the central co-ordinate of the planet?

Lee: Our scanners indicate a large iceberg, in fact, it's an ice palace. It appears to be where central communications are coming from on the planet.

Captain: Take us there, Sanchez.
The planet surface of Icarus 5

Actors 2, 4 & 5 *Create the Ice Palace with the doors opening, whilst Sanchez and the Captain stand apart from them on the imaginary roof of the shuttle craft.*

50

Actors 2, 4 & 5: (_Now morph into the Icarunian of half-bird - half-reptile, multi-rolling, and speaking as one_) We told you to leave us in peace. Leave at once.

Captain: Look just relax, I'm here to make a deal.

Actors 2, 4 & 5: (_Multi Rolling, speaking as one_) We want no deal. Leave at once.

Captain: Shhh, shhh. (He _puts his fingers to his lips to silence them._) Listen to me, will you? You should be praising me for what I'm trying to do down here. You're gonna be rich beyond your wildest dreams.

Actor 2: (_Multi Rolling._) Your mind demonstrates your egos have outgrown your bodies' development.

Captain: Ya kidding me, look at you? You're prehistoric. Why, you don't have the brains you were born with.

Actor 4: (_Multi Rolling._) A long time ago, our ancestors had these primal thoughts, with threats and inept actions. This created a divided society. We have since evolved as one. You will have to learn to try again and develop as one with the planets.

Sanchez: Shall we blast them, Captain..?

Actors 2, 4 & 5: Create a dome around Sanchez and the Captain.

Captain/Sanchez: Ahhhh what's happening?

Actors 2, 4 & 5: _Bring their raised arms down on the Captain and Sanchez reducing them in size to small children._

Sanchez: We're shrinking.

Captain: Is this a hoax? What you doing to us? This isn't fair... I want my mummy.

Sanchez: I'm scared... I want my, daddy.

Captain: Ah, shut up about your, daddy, I want my, daddy.

Sanchez: My, daddy's, bigger than your, daddy.

Captain: My, daddy's richer than your daddy.

Sanchez: Oh, no he's not.

Captain: Oh, yes, he is.

Actors 2, 4, & 5: *Standing, back on the bridge of the 'Starship of Freedom'.*

Imani: Message coming in from Icarus 5. The Captain and Navigator Sanchez have been returned to their original childhood state. They're to live out their life again with the prospect of learning from their mistakes. It's to make a better development for the future. The Icarunian's have asked if we can beam them back on board?

Lee: 'We know what we are but know not what we may be'

Imani: Officer Lee, I don't understand. Is that an instruction, what do you mean?

Lee: An interesting lesson from the Icarunian's, giving the Captain and Sanchez the ultimate gift... of time and evolution. This time to be used wisely. Yes, Imani, beam them up from the planet surface... to the ships ... Creche!

~

Lydon Price's Monologue

Lydon Price is now in the ship's Creche.

I been in this playroom and it's not fair. Why has, Sanchez, got all those toys, why can't I play with his? He's got more than me. What, share mine with him? He's not playing with my toys... Why? Because. They're mine! What, put them away? It's not even bedtime yet, and anyway I can leave them here on the floor... yeah. Okay, okay, so you keep telling me, if I put them away, I'll know where they are when I want them... But I know where they are... they're here on the floor, right in front of me! Ahhh, now you're telling me it's time for bed... I don't wanna wake up strong and healthy. I wanna stay here playing with my toys. Anyway, where's my supper? I'm hungry. What do you mean 'learn to be patient'? I am patient, ask anyone. I'm the most patient boy in the whole creche. In fact, the other creche worker said they'd never seen a boy... ever, ever... so patient as me'... Don't just take my word for it, ask anyone. Okay okay, ask Sanchez? There you are, Sanchez, you're not a loser anymore. You can play with that toy... Oh, I am being a good boy...Thank you. How does it feel to be nice...? Ermm...

~

53

Tasks

Speaking and listening
Task 1: Discuss how accents could be used to improve characterisation. Consider intonation, tone, volume, and pauses. What difference would that make to the interpretation of the play? Discuss how the movement of the characters could be enhanced with proxemics *(the positions of actors in relation to one another.)* How would you show who was in charge and their status on the 'Starship of Freedom? **Task 2**: Rehearse the play again, adding accents and proxemics to push the boundaries of the play as far as possible.

Reading
Think about the lines *'Gotcha Commodore. No one knows diplomacy better than I do. We are shortly entering their solar system? They'll be no threat, over.'* Is this statement correct from Captain Price? **Task 1**: Read the dialogue of Captain Price and make a note of the lines, where we find the opposite outcomes through his hypocrisy. *(He's implying he has noble beliefs to the Commodore, but what is he really thinking and what he is actually intending to do?)*

Lithium (Li):
Lithium is the lightest metal on earth. Found in batteries, it is used to power many electrical products, such as smartphones and electric cars. As demand for lithium increases, the harmful effects of lithium mining impacts communities, making it difficult for them to access water. Current levels of lithium recycling are extremely low. Only around 5% of the lithium-ion batteries sold in the EU are recycled while the rest are sent to landfill or incinerated. This increases the need to mine even more lithium. Until the collection and recycling of metals like lithium is made compulsory, today's wasteful practices will have widespread, negative consequences for the environment and society. The demand for lithium is rising because it converts chemical energy into electrical energy very efficiently.

Scientists believe that rechargeable lithium-ion (Li-ion) batteries offer the greatest potential for tomorrow's energy storage systems. As a result, demand

54

will increase in order to power personal electronic goods, energy storage systems and electric vehicles. The high-quality lithium needed for this is mainly accessible in just a few South American countries, such as Chile and Bolivia – it is these countries that are most likely to be affected by continued lithium mining.

Writing

Captain Price and Sanchez are given a moral lesson and the opportunity to learn from their mistakes and make a fresh start. What would you change, if you had the opportunity to alter a self-destructing world? Read the article above: Lithium has always created controversy, potentially poisoning water tables but it is necessary for mobile phone manufacturing. Coal, nuclear fuel and gas are also controversial power sources. **Task 1:** Write a formal speech, arguing against the use of these fuels and present it to a small group or to your teacher.

Extension Task: Watch the clip to learn about what makes a clear and informative report.
https://www.bbc.co.uk/bitesize/articles/znc26v4

6. Anxiety Attack

Characters

*Characters' names can be switched on gender.
Take your pick, just remember to change the pronouns.*

Sammy
Steve - Dad
Toni - Mum
Aunt Karin or Uncle Ken

Scene: Saturday morning Mum, Dad and Sammy, are in the Kitchen, Aunt Karin has just arrived.

Aunt Karin: Morning everybody, thought I'd just pop round. Phew, it's freezing out there. How's everyone? *(Silence, a long awkward pause.)*

Mum: Hi, Karin, we're alright, aren't we ..? (Confused, *looking at Dad and Sammy.)*

Dad: I suppose so.

Mum: How are you, Karin?

Aunt Karin: Fine, But it's a bit chilly in here. What's up, have I come at the wrong time?

Dad: Well… would you like to tell your Auntie Karin what's up then, Sammy?

Mum: She's been sent her school report.

56

Dad: If I'd have got a report like this from school when I was your age, I would have been grounded for a week. I'd be ashamed of it, and you should be too.

Sammy: I can't help it if I get things wrong, can I? I'm just no good at picking things up.

Dad: You're telling me.

Mum: Oh, give it a rest, Steve. But, Sammy, you'll soon be sitting your GCSEs.

Aunt Karin: She's only in Year 8!

Dad: Yeah, well, she just stays in her room playing on those stupid games... or if not, playing on her phone till all hours. No wonder she can't learn anything or do anything. I mean, what happened to football on a Saturday morning? How come, you don't play that now?

Flashback to six months ago, Sammy is playing football with mum, dad and Aunt Karin on the touchline. Dad is running and shouting instructions, whilst Sammy is reacting to the dialogue in slow motion. She is facing the audience.

Mum: Come on, Sammy!

Dad: That's it, Sammy, take her on, take her on, now pass it, pass it. Oh, too slow, too slow.

Aunt Karin: Never mind, Sammy, you're doing fine, just keep trying.

Sammy: (*Speaking a direct address to the audience.*) Trying? I am trying, but I'll never get past that centre half.

Dad: Come on, Sammy, stop daydreaming, you should be chasing that ball, run!!!

57

Mum: You're shouting again, Steve. *(Shouting.)* Come on, Sammy!

Dad: What's up with her? This is the third Saturday in a row, she's just not playing like she used to, I don't know, just too indecisive.

Aunt Karin: Calm down, Steve, you're going to give yourself a heart attack the way you're carrying on. Let, Sammy, play her own game.

Dad: Oh, don't you start, Sis. What do you know about football?

Mum: Steve's right, Karin, he never misses 'Match of the Day.' do you love?

Dad: I certainly know more about football than those, Pundits, that's for sure.

Mum: Look, the referees awarded a penalty, Sammy, normally takes them, do your mum proud love. Come on, Sammy. *(Sammy mimes being tackled and rubbing her leg.)*

Aunt Karin: I think she's hurt though; she's rubbing her leg. It might be better if someone else takes it.

Dad: No.no. She's the penalty taker, come on, get up, Sammy.

Sammy: *(Direct address.)* If I hold my leg long enough, they'll think I'm hurt, they can give it to someone else. *(She carries on rubbing her leg.)* Oh no, now they're telling me I'm fine, but I'm not fine. If I take the kick, I'll mess it up.

Mum: I knew it, she's up and rubbing it off, nice one, Sammy.

Dad: Good, Okay, Sammy, you know what to do with it.

Sammy: *(Direct address as she places an imaginary ball on the penalty spot facing the audience.)* Oh no, Do I really have to take it? I want to get

58

out of here, I can't breathe and I feel sick. Everyone's looking at me, I can't do it, I just can't do it. It never used to bother me, but now? Do I kick it right or left? I can't do it. Maybe the goalie will move and I can kick it down the middle? The goals look so small… and the keeper looks massive… Oh no, I'm gonna miss it. *(She misses it.)*

Dad: Ohhh nooo.

Sammy: I knew it. *(Hangs her head in embarrassment.)*

Dad: *(Shouting at Sammy.)* There's the ball, there's the net, put the ball in the net, what part of that don't you get!

Present time back in the kitchen.

Aunt Karin: Maybe you'll feel like playing again, Sammy, when the times right.

Dad: I just don't understand why you've packed in football?

Mum: Yes love, I thought you enjoyed a good kick about.

Dad: Too busy with your face on that phone screen.

Mum: Well, it certainly isn't in your school exercise books!

Aunt Karin: I'm sure, Sammy's, trying her best. These are different times, difficult challenges.

Dad: You're not wrong there, Karin, there's some difficult challenges on this report *(He starts reading it.)* 'Avoids asking questions.' 'Can be prone to excuses with uncompleted tasks.' 'Attendance concerns.'

Mum: Your dad's not wrong, Sammy, you used to love going to school, you never had a day off. You even enjoyed doing those

59

private lessons after school, so you could sit that grammar school entrance exam text.

Flashback to the day of the results of the entrance exam test:

Sammy: *(Direct address.)* It was waiting for me on the table when I got home, the letter. The decision, to pass or fail for a grammar school, in or out?

Dad: Well, come on, Sammy, we've been waiting for you to open it.

Mum: Oh, we're so excited aren't we love?

Dad: We certainly are, come on, open it!

Sammy: *(Direct address.)* All of a sudden, I couldn't breathe, I just looked at the letter and I couldn't stop shaking. It was like when I'd looked at the questions on the exam paper, feeling pressured, like my brain was going to explode. I knew the answers, but I froze … And now with the letter in my hand, it was like something awful was about to happen, and it did.

Dad: *(Dad snatches the letter off Sammy and reads it out.)*
Unfortunately, we cannot offer you a place at our grammar school… I'm very disappointed in you, Sammy, I expected more of you. *(Under his breath.)* Well, that was a waste of time, having those private lessons.

Mum: And all that money… tut.

Sammy: I spoke to, Aunt Karin, on the phone.
Flashback to the phone call.

Aunt Karin: I'm sure you did your best, Sammy, you can't do any more than that. I know your, dad's upset, but that is not your problem.

60

Sammy: But I failed, Aunt Karin, I was so nervous I could hardly write my name on the exam paper, I couldn't... I just couldn't get started.

Aunt: Ok, Sammy, take a few deep breaths and slow down. Just tell me about these nerves and how do they feel when they start?

Sammy: I just feel so scared, like I know I'm gonna fail, everything seems so confusing.

Aunt Karin: Ok, Sammy, I get that. What's going on inside you, how does it feel?

Sammy: Oh, Aunt Karin, it's awful. My heart starts beating faster and faster and my stomach is in knots, like butterflies but worse. I start getting hotter, sweating and my mouth goes dry, worse still I start struggling to breathe.

Aunt Karin: Whatever this is, Sammy, it's stopping you from living your life and doing what you want to do. I'll make enquiries with a health professional and then I'll have a word with your mum and dad, how does that sound?

Sammy: Yes... please.

Present.

Mum: Anxiety?

Dad: Don't talk wet, I've never heard anything so ridiculous in all my life. You need to grow a thicker skin, that's all, like me!

Mum: I think your, dad's, right honey. Your, Aunt Karin's, been listening to too many of these news reports and social worker types.

Dad: Yeah, they seem to have a diagnosis for everything these days… even laziness.

Sammy: *(Direct address.)* Apart from, Aunt Karin, no one seemed to listen to me. It was the same in my History lesson at school. I was asked by my, teacher 'Why did, cavemen run or fight?' I thought about my fears, how they increased when I thought I was in danger and how I wanted to run. But, also my fears could protect me and I wanted to tell the class, but… I didn't. I just said, I agreed with the others in the group, who said, 'How would we know what cavemen thought, Sir.'

Dad: So, what are we going to do about this report or are you going to ignore it like everything else?

Aunt Karin: Steve, Toni, will both of you listen? We've discussed this before; I think Sammy needs your support with this issue.

Mum: But how are you so certain it's anxiety?

Aunt Karin: I'm not a trained psychologist, but all the symptoms Sammy is experiencing sound like anxiety. It's stopping her from doing what she really wants to do… and that is to achieve.

Dad: Will you listen to yourself? I've never heard such nonsense.

Aunt Karin: Steve, remember that time when you and I were at school together and you were playing football. Dad always used to push you to be a better player and maybe turn professional in the future.

Dad: You know as well as me, I wasn't big enough. I was getting smashed each game.

Aunt Karin: Dad, was always pushing you, questioning why you weren't training. Do you remember that? I'm sure you do… and why you weren't playing to your best.

62

Dad: Look, it's more about, Sammy, facing up to her responsibilities. I had to do that when I was her age… like, even in my option choices at school, between what I wanted and what dad wanted and even then, I… even… I just wish… I'd

Mum: You wish, you'd done what Steve?

Dad: Wished I'd… nothing, Toni. Can we leave this…please?

Aunt Karin: Don't you see it, you're living your life through, Sammy's, just as dad tried to live his life through you. You're not thinking of what, Sammy, really wants.

Dad: Yeah, but.

Mum: Maybe your sister, could be right on this one, Steve, maybe we should look into it?

Dad: *(Puts his head down, feeling shamed.)* Such as doing what?

Aunt Karin: I've done some research. With early intervention, you can empower, Sammy, to understand anxiety, so she'll know how to manage it. To learn from and explore the triggers and symptoms. But with support in place.

Mum: Actually, that's not a bad idea. I'll bet they even have school counselling to help students with this. Come on, Steve?

Dad: Don't you think this is a bit extreme?

Aunt Karin: From what I've read, it can lead to social isolation, which can get worse as she gets older.

Dad: Really?

Aunt Karin: I don't want to repeat your words…. but…

Sammy: *(Direct address.)* And so for the first time, we can talk about my feelings as a family. It's good to be listened to and not to feel criticized. I'm beginning to understand how my fears affect my ability to perform in pressured situations. I now have the support of a school councillor, who's taught me to 'name and tame' my emotions. I don't beat myself up, certainly, not as much with negative thoughts. I'm now feeling more confident in my ability to cope and starting to play football again. And guess what, Aunt Karin? … it's fun…

Sammy is now back on the imaginary football pitch taking a penalty. She carefully places the ball on the spot, stands back, grounded and takes a deep breath. She is determined as she assesses the goalkeeper and picks her spot in the corner. The goals are massive and the keeper is tiny…. she smiles confidently to herself and starts the run-up to kick the ball…

Sammy: Yesssss… *(As the ball hits the net, she jumps up and punches the air.)* Bring it on!

~

Aunt Karin's Monologue

Aunt Karin is talking to her sister-in-law, Toni.

Toni, I don't know if Steve ever mentioned it to you, but he was interested in creative subjects at school, specifically art. He was brilliant at it and he loved it. He spent most of his lunchtime in the art room, even when he was meant to be training for football. He wanted to study art at university and his teachers knew how gifted he was and so did most of his peers. My dad wouldn't let him go. He said the only artists that make money are dead artists … and it'll be no use to you then. He said art's a hobby, not a real job and that you can do a course in engineering. There's always employment in that area. Reluctantly, Steve agreed to it and now he's working… doing a job, that he doesn't like… He threw all his artwork on the tip and has never painted since. I know deep down, he's always resented dad for that. What's worse, he carries it on with that 'just get on with it, don't complain attitude.' Sometimes, I think he's moulded in the same way. It's an intergenerational thing… Apart from today… it was the first time I've seen him accept that, Sammy needs help with her own wants and expectations. He actually started listening to her… Anyway, will you give him this? *(She hands Toni a new boxed painting set)* You never know, he might even start painting again. Perhaps, make it into a real job… this time.

~

Tasks

Speaking and listening
In the play 'Anxiety Attack' the family look at the issues and needs of Sammy at various stages in life. Discuss Sammy's needs in pairs or as a group. **Task 1:** Write a list of questions that TV hosts might ask if they were to present a talk show where the focus of discussion is on 'Anxiety' **Task 2:** Discuss or improvise flashbacks to various moments in Sammy's life that are not mentioned in the play, e.g., the first day at high school, going on school camp, school nativity play, etc. What impact did these moments have on Sammy? **Task 3:** Multi-roll as presenters and act out on a split screen *(Split the stage into two areas.)* In groups, rehearse and perform to the rest of the class.

Reading
The use of negativity, irony, exaggeration or ridicule is exposed through Sammy's father's comments, particularly in the context of his own shortcomings. Highlight the negative statements he makes to pick out Sammy's flaws. **Task 1:** Make a list of positive statements he could have said. What impact might that have made in helping improve Sammy's confidence?

Writing
Thinking of Sammy's dad and looking back on his childhood, we see him realising his own mistakes. **Task 1:** Write an informal letter of apology from the father to Sammy. Explain his errors from the past and how his behaviour might have influenced Sammy's. Explain, also, how he intends to change this in the future. Think about how he would set the right tone *(so it seems friendly, apologetic and natural.)*.

Extension Task: Look at the informal approaches to letter writing. Then research:
https://www.bbc.co.uk/bitesize/guides/z996hyc/revision/3

66

7. I Saw it, Yes.

Characters
Actor 1
Actor 2
Actor 3
Actor 4

Scene: *Staging of the actor's choice.*

Actor 1: On the bus.

Actor 2: They called her fat.

Actor 3: She was eating a cake.

Actor 4: They pushed it in her mouth.

Actor 1: She burst into tears.

Actor 2: Click.

Actor 3: It went online.

Actor 4: Just a bit of fun.

All Actors: I saw it, yes.

Actor 1: Baby boy all alone.

Actor 2: Such a loser.

Actor 3: Mum and dad split up.

Actor 4: He broke down in class.

Actor 1: Lashed out at us.

Actor 2: Click.

Actor 3: It went online.

Actor 4: Not my fault.

All Actors: I saw it, yes.

Actor 1: She hadn't eaten a thing all day.

Actor 2: A religious thing.

Actor 3: They pushed food under her nose.

Actor 4: She had a fight.

Actor 1: We gathered round.

Actor 2: Click.

Actor 3: It went online.

Actor 4: I just happened to be there.

All Actors: I saw it, yes.

Actor 1: She stroked her hand.

Actor 2: She told her she was in love.

Actor 3: They called her out for it.

Actor 4: Who are you?

Actor 1: What are you?

Actor 2: Click.

Actor 3: It went online.

Actor 4: What's it to do with me?

All Actors: I saw it, yes.

Actor 1: He wanted to fit in.

Actor 2: He joined a gang.

Actor 3: Should have been warned.

Actor 4: He carried a blade.

Actor 1: Left bleeding in the park.

Actor 2: Click.

Actor 3: It went online.

Actor 4: He wouldn't listen.

All Actors: I saw it, yes.

Actor 1: She has this accent.

Actor 2: She's not from here.

Actor 3: Mixes her words.

Actor 4: Mimicked her words.

69

Actor 1: Lashed out hurt.

Actor 2: Click.

Actor 3: It went online.

Actor 4: I didn't think it bothered her.

All Actors: I saw it, yes.

Actor 1: They wave our flag.

Actor 2: Speeches of hate.

Actor 3: The chosen ones.

Actor 4: Divide and separation.

Actor 1: Sharing messages of hate.

Actor 2: Click.

Actor 3: It went online.

Actor 4: Best to ignore it.

All Actors: I saw it, yes.

Actor 1: Am I to blame?

Actor 2: I didn't send the posts.

Actor 3: I didn't intervene.

Actor 4: I'm on my own.

70

Actor 1: It's not my fault.

Actor 2: But there's more of us?

Actor 3: We should have stood for all of us.

Actor 4: It went online.

All Actors: We all saw it, yes … but?

~

Actor 1 Monologue

The dog can be on an imaginary lead.

I saw it, yes. It was on its daily walk. Been stuck in all night, cooped up most of the day. The 5 minute walk… drag… down the road on its lead, no it wasn't a lead, it was a belt, always done reluctantly. The owner wanted to get back home as quickly as possible, get in from the rain and get to work. 'Stop that sniffing!' Yank. A pull on the lead 'Yelp!' as her paws lift off the pavement and bounce hard on the concrete. The excitement of the road to freedom slipping fast. She tried to sniff an oncoming Labrador. 'Pack it in.' Yank. She tried to relieve herself on the traffic post, well, we all have to go sometimes. 'What have I told you?' Yank. And then he tripped over her lead. Yessss, serves him right… but noooo. He's pulled off the lead and holds it above her head. I felt helpless. Sick. Would anyone stop him? I looked around and everyone carried on walking. They must have seen it? Heard it? As it came down on her, 'Yelp.' I needed someone with me, to lessen the load… no one. No one. 'Yelp.' I stood there helpless, watching, tears running down my eyes and then… I shouted… NO!

~

Tasks

Speaking and listening.
Task: Read the poem out loud, two or three times, then discuss how you could perform it. Consider: adding sound effects, adding a chorus, experimenting vocally, repeating some parts, improvising scenes in the poem, adding still images, **Task 2:** Rehearse and create a presentation to the group or the class. Think about adding a personal statement of your own to conclude the performance.

Reading.
Task: Taking a closer look at the script. How is it structured? Why is it structured this way? What is the main message of the script and why is it important for us to question the incidents that have been witnessed? What is identity and what does it make you think of? Share your ideas in pairs and then as a class.

Writing.
Task: 'History repeats itself if we do not learn from the past,' Think about this statement and then write an essay arguing whether you agree or disagree with it.
To help, create a planning grid of 6 equal size boxes in which you organise your ideas. Each box should cover a separate idea that you can write a paragraph within your essay.

Extension Task: Look at the YouTube video on developing argumentative essays.
https://www.youtube.com/watch?v=oAUKxr946SI

Alternatively- Protest songs can be created to form a peaceful voice. Look at the link of the protest singer Buffy Sainte-Marie to get an insight into writing your own protest song.
https://www.youtube.com/watch?v=7mDvukMvttU

8. Taking My Ball Home

Characters' names can be switched on gender. Take your pick, just remember to change the pronouns.

Characters

Brook/Brooke a teenage boy/girl
Andy/Andi a teenage boy/girl
Mum/Dad
Mr/Miss Thornton, a teacher

Scene: Bedroom. Curtains drawn. Brook plays a computer game on a large screen.

Brook: (*Speaking a direct address to the audience.*) Do you ever get that feeling that it's just not fair? That you try your best and yet some people who don't try as hard as you or even are as good as you… somehow end up getting ahead of you? I mean what is that all about? You understand, don't you? I mean, it's just so annoying. It makes you think, what is the point in trying?

Mum enters the bedroom.

Mum: Are you coming down, Brook?

Brook: No, mum.

Mum: You've been up here on your own, for hours now.

Brook: I've just moved up to another level, I don't intend to lose it now.

74

Mum: But it's a lovely day outside and your curtains are drawn.

Brook: Stop bothering me, I need them drawn to see the screen.

Mum: What is it you're playing?

Brook: Death Warrior.

Mum: Looks very violent.

Brook: Everyone my age is playing it, even younger kids… Gotcha. *(Hitting the keypad.)*

Mum: Well, I don't like it. Come on, Brook, you've been up here every night for the past two weeks. Your dad and I have hardly seen you. We're getting worried about you.

Brook: Oh, stop fussing over me and leave me alone, I just want to play my game.

Mum: And that's another thing, your attitude, it's changed. Is it because of these stupid games you keep playing every evening? Anyway, I want it off, I'm giving you 10 minutes, no more.

She leaves.

Brook: Do I have to?

Mum: Yes, 10 minutes, no more.

Brook: *(Direct address.)* See what I mean? I come up here, to get out of their way and still I get constant harassment. I just want to be left alone in my bedroom. I don't want to involve myself in other people's things. I just want to play my game, it's virtual you see, I can't hurt them, and nobody can hurt me. Gotcha, great shot, took him down by the legs.

Mum: Andy's, here.

Brook: I'm busy, Mum… *(Direct address.)* But I know he's going to come up regardless and winge about, why, I didn't meet him in the park.

Mum: He's on his way up.

Brook: *(Direct address.)* What did I tell you!

Andy: Hi, Brook. What you up to?

Brook: Nothing.

Andy: What happened? I've been waiting for you at the park.

Brook: I never said I was going… for certain.

Andy: But you did say you were coming… Have I said something wrong to you, or something? You're normally reliable, when you say 'Yes' you mean it?

Brook: *(Direct address.)* Oh, here we go again, lecture number two about to start, telling me I'm letting everyone down. *(He turns to talk to Andy.)* Just give it a rest, Andy.

Andy: Are you coming to drama club tomorrow, you like that?

Brook: Oh, I don't think so, a load of kids pretending to be trees.

Andy: That's hilarious, Brook, *(Sarcastically.)* Anyway, everyone was asking where you were last week, you're good at acting.

Brook: Tell that to, Thornton.

Andy: How do you mean?

Brook: He just picks his favourites.

Andy: Is that why you're annoyed... because you didn't get one of the lead roles in the school production?

Brook: No...

Andy: But they offered you a part in the chorus, same as me, plus you've been given quite a few lines and they're really funny ones.

Brook: Be serious,

Andy: So, have you told them you're not going to be in it?

Brook: Too right, I wouldn't be in that show, even if they paid me.

Andy: But even small parts are just as important... Is that why you were messing about in his English lesson this afternoon?

Brook: Well, you were there, I wasn't messing about. He's just picking on me now, because, I said I'm not doing the show. *(Direct address.)* Yeh, too right I was messing about, he's messed up my plans, so I'll mess up his.

Andy: What did he say to you after the class had gone?

Brook: You know, same old thing, 'Stop interrupting, get on with your work' He's just got it in for me these days... And something about smiling, what's that all about?

Flashback to the end of Mr Thornton's lesson with Brook.

Mr Thornton: Brook, you've had constant reminders to stay on task, it's not like you to disrupt the class. What's going on?

Brook: It wasn't me though, Sir.

Mr Thornton: Ok, perhaps it wasn't you, but why do you seem so angry lately? Is it an expression of failing, on my part?

Brook: I don't know what you mean? *(Direct address.)* Of course, it's your fault, you just didn't notice me, but you do now!

Mr Thornton: Well, how do you feel about the school production?

Brook: I'm not bothered about it.

Mr Thornton: Is that because you didn't get the part you wanted from the auditions?

Brook: No… *(Direct address.)* James Collinson as the lead role? Ha, don't make me laugh. He's as wooden as a fence post. You could hammer nails in him!

Mr Thornton: Well, your face doesn't tell me that. In drama club, you were always smiling and happy. weren't you?

Brook: I suppose so.

Mr Thornton: Do people smile back at you now, Brook?

Brook: I'm not bothered, Sir.

Mr Thornton: But do they, Brook?

Brook: No, Sir.

Mr Thornton: Don't you realise, Brook, that when you smiled, the whole world was smiling back at you. The world is a reflection of you.

Brook: But, I don't feel like smiling.

78

Mr Thornton: Is this down to, James, getting the part you wanted?

Brook: No… but it's not fair that he got it.

Mr Thornton: When people audition for a role, we are looking for someone suitable for the character we have in mind.

Brook: Well, how can you compare him with me? *(Direct address.)* Everyone thinks I'm better than him at acting… Ask anyone?

Mr Thornton: It's also true that comparison is the 'Thief of joy' and you must realise that not accepting the decision is an act of self-harm on your side.

Brook: It's not right, it makes me look like a failure, why should I fail?

Mr Thornton: No, Brook, you haven't, it's just a **F**irst **A**ttempt **I**n **L**earning. Turn this into a success by honing your skills, defining your roles with the tools you acquire in the drama club after school. You don't think every actor gets every part they go for do you? They have to also strengthen their own resilience.

Brook: Well, some people get success without putting the work in?

Mr Thornton: That's true, Brook, but a lot of them end up getting exposed for it. Don't take a TV reality show as a model for your success. Most people have to put the work in to succeed.

Brook's bedroom.

Andy: And what did you say then?

Brook: I said, I'd think about it. *(Still playing the game on the screen.)*

79

Andy: So… are you coming to the drama club tomorrow?

Brook: I'll think about it.

Mum: *(Enters the room.)* Are you coming down, Brook?

Brook: I'll think about it.

Andy: Are you coming to the park then?

Brook: I'll think about it after I've finished this game.

Andy: *(Getting frustrated and ready to go.)* Don't think about it too much, Brook, because I want to go and play in the real world.

Brook: *(Direct address.)* Maybe I am trying hard... hard to compromise. I hate it when adults are right, but I hate it, even more, when my friends are right too. It's hard enough hurting yourself, even harder knowing that I'm hurting others. *(Brook, pulls back the curtains and turns to Andy.)* Look at that, it's sunny outside. Come on then, Andy, what do you fancy, nets or penalty taker?

~

80

Mr Thornton's Monologue

Mr Thornton is writing Brook's report, thinking about it and reading it out loud.

Interesting one this… mmm let me think about it… *(Mr Thornton looks up, pauses for a moment and then begins.)* Brook has an excellent understanding of the drama conventions studied over the past year. He is making good progress and knows how to integrate creative ideas successfully into performance. He has produced some outstanding practical work and mostly works well with his peers. Brook is confident and wants to succeed in each assessment. I was, however, disappointed with Brook's attitude and his commitment towards our end-of-year school production. We have since spoken at length about this and he has, consequently, demonstrated the determination needed to turn disappointment into success. Furthermore, he has developed his interpretive understanding of character-based work with good vocal technique and experimental physicality in rehearsal. This has helped to develop his emotional skills in a more mature manner. He now approaches each task with an eye for detail and concentration, adapting to acting and reacting in character in each task set for him. I look forward to more improvements next year.

~

Tasks

Speaking and listening
In this play, Brook uses a direct address. This is also called 'breaking the fourth wall', a term used by the practitioner, Bertolt Brecht. *(The fourth wall is the theatrical term for the imaginary wall that exists between actors on stage and the audience. The actors pretend they cannot hear or see the audience. The direct address breaks this illusion.)* He then turns to other characters to continue the conversation as though they haven't heard his thoughts between his direct address. **Task 1:** Write a short scene for a play where you fail at something and then, determinedly, turn it around, demonstrating resilience through adding a direct address to the audience.

Reading
Reading the section where Thornton talks to Brook, look for the negative responses from Brook. Who is he blaming? What could he do differently? **Task 1:** Using each letter of your name, write down positive words about yourself. These can be something you are good at or something you like about yourself.

Writing
Imagine Brook in the future as a successful actor. **Task 1:** Create a newspaper report of him/her giving an interview of their life, entitled 'How I became resilient and didn't give in.' Using your imagination, recount stories of how resilience was used to improve him/her as a person.

Extension Task: A 'snowflake' is a derogatory slang term for a person who is perceived to have a sense of entitlement or is over-sensitive to comments about them. How accurate is this article? Do you think this is biased or exaggerated? Write two detailed paragraphs on the positive and negative aspects of this story.
https://www.independent.co.uk/life-style/snowflake-meaning-definition-gammon-piers-morgan-trump-b737499.html

9. The Bully

Characters

John - Victim
Jack - Victim
Jake - Victim
Bruce - Bully and eldest by 2 years

John, Jack and Jake are all aspects of one person's personality. They are walking towards a bus stop. Bruce, a bully, is waiting there.

John: Oh no, look who it is! Bruce is there, heads down guys.

Jack: I'm not scared of him. If he says 'owt, I'll give him something to laugh about.

Jake: C'mon guys, just ignore him, he's not worth it. He's only doing it for a reaction.

John: Yeah, he's not worth it.

Bruce: Well, well, well what have we got here then? Three fat sausages sizzling in a pan.

Jake: Ha, ha. just like Shakespeare you are, Bruce. The bard of the bus stop. *(Sarcastic.)*

John: Don't provoke him, Jake, you'll only make it worse.

Bruce: Have you got something to say?

Jack: Have you got something to say?!

John: Please don't, Jack, you know what he's like.

Bruce: Listen to the little piggy, Jack, or you'll wish you stayed at home.

Jack: Oh yeah, we'll see about that! *(John and Jake hold Jack back.)*

Jake: He's a few pence short of a quid, Jack, leave him be. He's used to his own company from what I've heard.

John: Yeah, he's not worth the bother, Jack, take the high ground.

Bruce: C'mon then, Jack, show us what you've got… in your lunchbox! *(Laughing.)*

Jake: What's your problem? What have we ever done to you? You're two years' older than us… physically.

John: Don't engage him, Jake. C'mon guys, let's just wait over here until the bus comes. We're wasting our time with him.

Jack: What goes around comes around, Bruce, mark my words.

Bruce: Oh yeah? I'll believe that when I see it.

Jack: You wouldn't see it if you'd stood in it.

(John, Jack and Jake move away from Bruce. Bruce calls his friends on his mobile phone and recounts the story to them jokingly.)

John: What is that guy's problem with me?

Jake: It's not just you, John, it's all of us. I'm not surprised he's got no mates.

Jack: He hates me as well; I never have known why.

John: He's got no mates?

84

Jake: Yeah, from what I've heard from my cousin.

(Laughter from Bruce on the phone.)

Bruce: Then I said, show us what you've got… in your lunchbox! Ha ha!

Jack: I'll tell you what though, one day he's gonna get his comeuppance and I, for one, would love to see it.

John: But he's older than us. What can we do?

Jake: We could tell a teacher? Drag his parents up to school on an evening. His dad works shifts as a fireman, I bet he'd be livid.

John: I've told my form tutor loads of times and it's come to nothing. You've got more chance of winning the lottery than expecting help from them.
(Bruce's phone starts ringing whilst he's pretending to be on a call with a friend. He panics and quickly puts the phone in his pocket.)

Jack: No, no, no I'm talking about real retribution, a lesson learnt that he'd never forget. A beating.

John: Yeah, I'd love to see that, Jack. Payback for all that he's given us.

Jake: That's not how the real world works boys. The weak get trodden underfoot. There's nothing we can do.

John: That car's coming fast up here!

Jack: Someone's late for work.

Jake: He must be going fifty.

(Screeching of tires, the car stops next to Bruce. He looks visibly upset and

85

protests his innocence through an audience direct address to the imaginary driver of the car.)

Bruce: I haven't done anything. No, I haven't. He said what? I wasn't even there then. No, I didn't. I would have never said that. Seriously. I don't even know what you're on about. With who? I don't even know him. Honestly. Oh please, please, I've just got it. Fine.

Bruce hands his mobile phone to the imaginary driver, he walks towards the others.

John: Oh no, this doesn't look good guys. He's really angry now. He's gonna hit us I can tell.

Jake: No, something's wrong here, he's almost crying.

Bruce: That's my dad over there. *(Muttering under his breath.)* And he tells me that one of you has said something about bullying… to a teacher, a teacher! Now when I find out which one it wa…

Jack: Looks like that's your old man, Bruce- and he doesn't look too happy. Now, how about I go up to him and tell him all the stuff that you've been saying to us.

Bruce: You dare say a word!

Jack: Oh, you're daring me? Ok then! *(Walking towards the car.)*

Bruce: Wait! *(Jack turns on his heels, arms crossed.)* What do you want from me?

Jack: Two things.

John: An apology.

Jake: And a promise.

86

Bruce: What promise?

Jake: That you'll never.

John: Ever.

Jack: Bully us again. 'Cause if you do, Bruce, we know who'll want to know about it.

Bruce: Fine. I'm sorry and I won't do it again. *(Muttering.)*

John: Say it again with meaning, so your dad can hear.

Bruce: I'm sorry and I won't do it again! *(Passive aggressively.)*

Jake: Why are you sorry?

Bruce: For making pig jokes.

Jack: Ok, if you're going to be stupi…

Bruce: Alright! I'm sorry for upsetting you. I'm sorry for all the things I've said. See dad, look I've apologized, can I have my phone back now?

The imaginary car drives off without giving Bruce his phone back. Bruce is holding back tears from running down his face.

Bruce: Oh now look what you've done. You guys are gonna get it big time now.

John: You promised, Bruce, you said you wouldn't bully us again. Please.

Jake: What a snake in the grass! We should've never listened to you… no one else does anyway!

87

Jack: You do know that we'll just tell your dad again. If he hears about this again, I doubt he'd be too happy.

John: Please, Bruce, we haven't said a thing to any teachers.

Bruce: He's working nights for two weeks. That gives me a fortnight to give you guys a pasting you'll never forget. I'm already grounded and now he's taken my phone.

John: Please, Bruce!

Bruce: Any last words?

Jack: Yeah.

Jake: He's behind you. *(Said in a pantomime voice.)*

Bruce: Dad, what are you doing here? No, I wasn't doing anything, we were just joking, you know, playing about! Weren't we guys? *(Bruce walks off with his imaginary dad, he casts back an angry look at Jack, Jake and John. As he is doing so, he slips on some dog mess and lands in it. He stands up and looks down in disgust at his hands.)* Oh, Noo!

Jack: I told you that you wouldn't see it if you'd stood in it, Bruce.

~

Bruce's Monologue

Bruce is sitting alone in his bedroom playing with a game console.

Sent to my room again, it's not like I've done much wrong. It's alright for John, Jack and Jake, they've got each other. I'm on my own but I don't care. I don't need friends; I prefer it that way. My parents think this is a punishment but they're wrong, they hardly talk to me anyway, except shouting at me and telling me to 'Be quiet.' Or 'Stop interrupting.' Because they're busy. Dad's got a promotion you see. He's a Station Officer and mum says he's got a lot of responsibility and emotional stress. Ha! What about my emotional stress, I've no mates, no one to talk to… just in here on my own. I did have a friend once, but he accused me of stealing his lousy game… so I hit him. This is the one. *(He is dismantling it.)* I heard my mum say to my dad that it was in my nature to be like this. I don't care anyway. What bothers me is my dad confiscating my phone, that's the most important thing to me right now… but who would I ring anyway?

~

Tasks

Speaking and Listening
Students are to read their own school statutory anti-bullying policy online or with copies of handouts. **Task 1:** Discuss their design and information for an advice leaflet on anti-bullying. **Task 2:** Improvise a scene where, Bruce, comes home from school, is he/she ignored, encouraged, neglected? Try to make a point about why, Bruce, bullies his peers? **Task 3:** Split into pairs, one play, Bruce, the other experiment in multirole as John, Jack and Jake. See if you can create different character personalities by speech, movement and gesture in this multi rolling task.

Reading
Make notes on the different personalities of the characters, who is the most aggressive in challenging, Bruce, consider the most peace-making approach or the most scared of him approach? **Task 1:** Make a list of the pros and cons of each approach?

Writing
How do you think, Bruce, is doing at school, has he been in trouble, and if so for what? What are his best and worst subjects? **Task 1:** Using formal writing skills, write his form tutors annual report, giving an overview of his behaviour and personality in school. An example is a monologue in the previous play 'Taking my ball home'.

Extension Task:
https://www.youtube.com/watch?v=XFmwWcGUWU4
This is a short clip on how to stop someone from bullying you. An extension task would be to write an essay on 'The impact of bullying in school'.

10. I Believe in Father Christmas

Characters.

Debbie – Mum
Pete – Dad
Charlotte/Charlie –
An older sibling
Joe/Joelle – Younger
sibling

Characters' names can be switched on gender. Take your pick, just remember to change the pronouns.

Scene: *Christmas Eve, Joe is knocking on Charlotte's bedroom door. She is busy on her phone.*

Charlotte: Go away.

Joe: What are you doing, Charlotte?

Charlotte: Go away.

Joe: Can I come in?

Charlotte: What part of 'Go away.' Don't you understand?

Joe: *(He walks in.)* I just want to see what you are doing.

Charlotte: What's it look like, stupid?

Joe: Don't call me, stupid, I don't like it.

Charlotte: Well, you are.

Joe: I still don't like it, Will you come sledging with me?

91

Charlotte: Can't you see I'm busy.

Joe: Doing what?

Charlotte: Shopping… I'm busy.

Joe: What are you shopping for?

Charlotte: Look, stop bothering me.

Joe: But what are you shopping for, it's, Christmas Eve?

Charlotte: I know it's, Christmas Eve, that's why I'm struggling with the same day delivery.

Joe: What are you trying to buy, who's it for?

Charlotte: Ahhhhh, just leave me alone you little rat, I'm trying to get this sorted.

Joe: Is it for me?

Charlotte: No, it's for mum and dad, I still haven't got them a present.

Joe: Why not?

Charlotte: Because… I've been busy, that's why not, so just shut up. Ah, at last. I've seen something … 'in a gift-wrapped box, guaranteed same day delivery' There's only one item available. That'll do, it's going to have to do. They've got everything they need anyway.

Joe: How you going to pay for it?

Charlotte: Dad said I can use his card; I'll pay him back.

Joe: When?

Charlotte: When I can afford it, but that's nothing to do with you.

Joe: I bet dad ends up paying for it… again.

Charlotte: Will you just shut up and leave me alone, I'm trying to get this sorted. (*She is typing hard on her phone screen.*)

Joe: Why are you getting so mad?

Charlotte: Because… because most of these stupid companies don't deliver on Christmas Day.

Joe: Father Christmas does on Christmas Day.

Charlotte: Oh, shut up about Father Christmas, he's not going to deliver this present on Christmas Day, it hasn't even left the warehouse yet.

Joe: He would do it if you asked him.

Charlotte: Don't be daft, surely you must know by now… he doesn't exist.

Joe: That's not true he does exist, he does.

Charlotte: Yeah right of course he does, he's going to come right down our chimney at midnight… As if!

Joe: He is, don't say that (*He starts to sob.*) he is coming tonight… Mum, Charlotte's being mean, she's saying, Father Christmas, isn't coming tonight (*He runs off to his mum.*)

Mum: Charlotte, why are you being so mean to your brother, you know he's looking forward to, Father Christmas. Don't ruin his excitement.

93

Charlotte: He needs to grow up.

Mum: No Charlotte, you need to grow up and be a bit more thoughtful.

Charlotte: I am thoughtful.

Mum: Well, give me a hand making this Christmas cake in the kitchen.

Charlotte: I'm busy mum, ask Joe. I've got my presents to sort out, they're not going to wrap themselves.

Mum: You've had weeks… in fact, months to sort this out. Why do you leave things to the last minute?

Charlotte: Oh, stop bothering me.

Mum: And stop being rude, the very least you could do is tidy your room, now sort it out, please.

Charlotte groans as she carries on with her phone. Later that afternoon there is a knock at the door, Charlotte runs to open it. She is disappointed as carol singers go into a burst of 'We wish you a Merry Christmas' played on audio cue or sung by dad in the wings.

Charlotte: Urgh, I thought you were someone else, *(Shouts and walks away.)* Mum!!!

Mum: *(Coming to the door as she addresses the imaginary singers.)* What a lovely surprise.

Joe: *(The singing stops.)* Isn't this great mum and… look it's starting to snow!

Mum: Can we make a small donation to your charity? *(Speaking to the imaginary carol singers.)* Thank you, goodbye and a Merry Christmas, to all of you.

Charlotte: Can someone close that door, it's sending a blast of cold air through the house?

Mum: Charlotte… the only blast of cold air coming through this house, is from your mouth. That was so rude, those carol singers are out collecting for the homeless

Charlotte: Huh… That's what they told you, I'll bet they keep for themselves.

Mum: In case you haven't noticed, this is a time when you show a generosity of spirit and see the best in everyone. You should try it.

Charlotte: Tut!

Mum: Though, I'm rapidly finding that difficult with you at the moment.

The doorbell rings again.

Charlotte: This is it, it's here. *(She runs to the door and opens it.)*

Dad: Someone's left the key in the door, I've been trying to get in and it's like the Arctic Circle out there! *(He walks in carrying a small dog under his arm in a towel.)*

Joe: Dad… You're home… Ahhh, you've got us a dog for Christmas, I can't believe it.

Mum: You haven't, have you, Pete?

Charlotte: Urgh, look at that scruffy mutt, I bet it's got fleas.

95

Dad: No, it's not for Christmas, I found it by the park and it belongs to someone.

Mum: How do you know?

Dad: I took it to the vet. They've said it's chipped and they're waiting for the owner to contact them. They asked if I could hold on to it till the owner collects it. Apparently, 'There's no room at the inn.' They're open, Christmas day, so it won't be for long.

Joe: Look, it's covered in snow, let's call her, 'Snowflake'

Dad: I'm pretty sure it's a he. *(He lifts it up.)*

Mum: Ahh, oh I see.

Joe: Can we make a bed for him by the Christmas tree, it smells so nice.

Charlotte: No... not when the fleabag starts leaving its own presents underneath it.

Mum: Let me get a towel and dry him. ... Ahh, look at those eyes, he looks so scared and lost but so lovely.

Joe: Oh, this is going to be the best Christmas ever!

Charlotte: I don't think so... *(Under her breath.)*

Very Late that same evening, Charlotte is on her phone with her friend.

Charlotte: Yeah, I know, it's not my fault, so unless this lazy courier arrives, I've got nothing for mum and dad... yeah, I know, what's the point of same-day delivery if they can't work, Christmas day... Hmm good point, I see what you mean. Yeah, I know it's late but I think they're in the kitchen wrapping presents. At least if I tell them now and not tomorrow morning, that'll soften the

96

blow about their present. I'll go and tell them now. Speak later. *(She puts the phone down and walks across to the kitchen, she is about to walk in but instead listens to the conversation behind the door.)*

Dad: How are you feeling, you must be exhausted?

Mum: *(Busy wrapping presents.)* Oh, I'm fine, it's just hectic putting the last few things together before tomorrow.

Dad: But you haven't stopped with all the overtime at work… and then here…

Mum: I'm sure it will be worth it, for a lovely Christmas together. I've hardly seen you … Are you ok?

Dad: Yes, just a little tired, it's just been busy at work. I picked up, Charlotte's new tablet by the way. It's all wrapped up ready for her.

Mum: You have got her the X50 haven't you?

Dad: Yes, it nearly broke the bank.

Mum: Well, with the overtime we've done, and cutting back on next year's holiday, we should have it paid off quite quickly. You've done so well, you're a good father.

Dad: You're an amazing mother too. Cheers *(They chink cups of tea.)* Come on, let's get some sleep, we'll be up with these presents early doors. I can hardly keep my eyes open, it's well past eleven… *(Joe is heard crying in the other room.)* What on earth is that noise?

In the next room, Joe has been asleep by the Christmas tree, he is cuddling 'Snowflake' He has just awoken and is looking for presents but there are none under the tree.

Joe: *(Crying loudly.)* He hasn't been, he hasn't been, have I been a bad boy? I didn't mean to be. Why hasn't he come?
Mum and dad walk into the room.

Dad: What on earth are you doing down here, Joe, you were upstairs in bed hours ago?

Joe: Father Christmas, hasn't been, he doesn't love me, I've got no presents… *(He is still sobbing.)* I should have stayed in bed.

Mum: How long have you been down here Joe?

Joe: I came down to say goodnight to, 'Snowflake' and we both waited for Father Christmas, but I fell asleep… and he's seen me waiting for him and he's left without leaving any presents.

Dad: Come here Joe. Don't cry, Father Christmas hasn't left… it's because he hasn't been… yet. It's only 11.30 pm! He doesn't come till after midnight.

Joe: Then, I haven't missed him?

Dad: No, *(Smiling.)* Not at all.

Mum: Come on Joe, you've got a big day tomorrow.

Joe (He puts his arms around mum and dad.) Sorry.

Dad: Let's go, up to your room.
Christmas morning and the whole family are by the tree.

Mum: look Joe, Father Christmas, has been and look what he's left us.

Joe: *(Screaming with delight.)* He's been, he's been. Look at what Father Christmas has brought me, Snowflake, I've got a car and a Nintendo. Oh, this is fantastic.

98

Dad: Merry Christmas, Debbie, you certainly deserve one.

Mum: And a merry Christmas to you too… and so many more together.

Dad: Merry Christmas, Charlotte, this is from your mother and I. *(They pass her the present.)*

Charlotte: Don't you mean Father Christmas?

Mum/Dad: Er, Yes. *(Confused.)*

Joe: What is it, Sis, can I look?

Charlotte: Come here Joe *(She puts her arm around him affectionately.)* Let's open it together… because I want to share this with you.

Mum/Dad: But it's your present, Charlotte.

Charlotte: Thanks, but it's ours… I want to share it, Father Christmas, can't afford two. *(They open it together.)* Er… Mum, Dad. This is from me to you both.
She passes over a present that is wrapped carefully, mum unwraps it and takes out a box. She opens it, lifts the lid and turns it upside down. There is nothing in it.

Mum: Is this a joke, Charlotte?

Charlotte: I wish it was. I've got you a present, but I left it till the last minute. It was meant to come same-day delivery but to be honest it has not arrived in time. I'm so sorry.

Mum: Well, what's with the empty box?

Charlotte: I want to tell you something. *(She starts to cry.)*

Dad: Charlotte, don't get upset, these things happen.

99

Charlotte: But Dad, I'm deeply sorry because I didn't think about it. I didn't think about you or mum. I just picked anything as long as it arrived on time. I've been so thoughtless, and I'll try so hard not to let that happen again.

Mum: But why the empty box?

Charlotte: I didn't realise how much both of you have done for me, I couldn't put into words how much I felt, so I blew 13 kisses into the box, one for every year of being together.

Mum: Come here, Merry Christmas, Charlotte. *(They all embrace.)* That's the best present ever.

A knock on the door.

Dad: I'll answer that, you never know it might be your courier. *(He goes to the door, answers it and returns to the family and picks up Snowflake in a towel.)* The owners have come for, Snowflake, they're here to collect him. *(He takes him out to the door.)*

Joe: Dad, do we have to give him back?

Mum: It's a time for giving, Joe, as well as receiving.

Charlotte: Come here, Joe. *(She holds his hand.)* He'll be happier with his own family, it's their Christmas present.

Dad: *(Returns holding a Christmas card.)* I've just had a lovely conversation with that family, they're so happy we found and looked after Snowflake, look what they've given us? *(He shows the card.)* It's the address of a Villa they own in Spain. They said we can go anytime we want, for a week. It's a thank you… a big thank you!

Mum: And we thought we were going to miss out on holidays this year.

100

Joe: Oh, this is going to be the best Christmas.

Charlotte: And the best, summer.

All: Ever.

~

Joe's Monologue

Characters' names can be switched on gender. Take your pick, just remember to change the pronouns.

Joe is Facetiming his Nan.

I'm using Charlotte's tablet, Nan. She said I could use it anytime I wanted. It's really good. She's been dead nice to me, even giving me hugs. It must be because it's Christmas! She even gave mum and dad a box of kisses. I thought they were going to cry; I think mum did. It's been a brilliant Christmas, Nan, but you'd never believe this, I thought Father Christmas wasn't going to come, I thought I'd missed him. You see, I waited up for him last night with 'Snowflake'. Oh, you don't know about 'Snowflake' do you? He's a dog that dad found in the park and he was covered in snow. We had to give him back though. He was so cute, I loved him. His owners came for him and I didn't want to give him back though but mum said I had to. I was upset at first but she said, Christmas is about giving as well as taking… I've always wanted a dog… do you think I should ask for one next Christmas? Mum said it's not a good idea, I don't know why? Anyway, you'd never believe it, Snowflake's owners said we could go on holiday to their house in Spain, oh it will be so good. Maybe you could come with us as well, Nan. I love you. Have a lovely Christmas.

~

102

Tasks

Speaking and listening
Christmas is not celebrated by everyone; this can be for various reasons, such as religion or beliefs. Christmas can be an enjoyable and yet also a very stressful time for many families. **Task 1**: Discuss in pairs or a group what Christmas means to you. What are the pros and cons of Christmas? What is Christmas time like for people who don't celebrate this religious celebration? **Task 2:** Improvise a comedic scene where the family are sitting down to eat their Christmas Dinner or opening their presents on Christmas Day. Alternatively, create a scene where a family doesn't celebrate Christmas and can't see what all the fuss is about.

Reading
In the play, Charlotte demonstrates selfish tendencies, **Task 1**: Read closely and make notes on her behaviour. Considering these notes, how do you think her family felt at the time? Do you think most teens behave in this way? Consider why it is so important to learn from mistakes and how they can prepare us for life in the future.

Writing
Doing something wrong and feeling guilty about it are common traits of growing up and developing as a human being. **Task 1:** Write a poem about someone you may have hurt and how that made you feel? Did you correct the hurt you inflicted? Start the story with the line 'When I looked in the mirror....' **Task 2:** Alternatively, write an uplifting poem about the joy and true spirit of Christmas that could be put in the centre of a seasonal celebration card.

Extension Task:
Performance poetry can be performed almost anywhere, but lately has developed a larger audience in festivals and concerts such as Glastonbury and T in the Park. It is fast becoming a staple diet of the entertainment circuit. Thanks to sites such as YouTube and SoundCloud, artists also share their voice and their work. Have a look and give it a go.

www.youtube.com/watch?v=wFCcbFtd6Zo

11. The Proposals

Style: Melodrama

Characters
Lord Vanity - The Boyfriend
Sir Ivan - The Villain
(Miss) Daphne - The Heroine
Lady Muck - The Mistress of the House
Gordon (The Gardener) - The Hero

Scene: Inside the house, Lady Muck is standing behind Miss Daphne adjusting her hair.

Lady Muck: There you are my angel; you look absolutely divine.

Daphne: Oh, do you really think so, mother?

Lady Muck: Of course, my dear, why there isn't a man in the country who would not wish to be your husband.

Daphne: Oh, mother, you really shouldn't say those things, I don't want just any man?

Lady Muck: Well, my dear, Lord Vanity, seems very fond of you indeed and he has that very large estate in the next village. It has delightful views over the sea, quite 'Des Res.'

Daphne: Yes, mother, but I can't say I'm awfully fond of him. By the way, he said he was coming to see me this afternoon.

Lady Muck: Daphne, it is just a matter of time before he asks for your hand in marriage my dear. It more depends on what he has in his other hand that will be the deciding matter, and let's hope it's lots of money.

Daphne: But mother, surely a marriage must be about love?

105

Lady Muck: Yes... love... and a healthy bank account, Daphne, my dear. One must not let standards drop and accept a proposal beneath your station.

Outside the door Gordon is standing with a bunch of flowers, he knocks.

Daphne: I'll get that mother, it might be, Lord Vanity?

She opens the door to Gordon the Gardener: he bows graciously to Daphne holding a bunch of flowers behind his back.

Gordon: Ma Lady, I've weeded the flower beds as you instructed and I couldn't resist cutting these for you. *(Gordan is suddenly sent flying to the floor by Lord Vanity with a wide sweeping gesture. Vanity has grabbed the flowers that were held behind Gordon's back. Gordan yelps!)* AHHHH! *(Vanity, now stood in Gordon's place, smirks and places the flowers in Daphne's hand. Gordon meantime is out cold and out of sight).*

Daphne: Oh, Lord Vanity, what a most wonderful surprise, the flowers are exquisite.

Lord Vanity: For you my darling, I would travel to 'The Hanging Gardens of Babylon.' if it were to bring a smile to that beautiful face.

Daphne: Why, Lord Vanity, you are a one with words, and good heavens you're making me blush.

Lord Vanity: My lady, I am a man of words, but I am also a man of action.

Daphne: My Lord, that's good to hear but what do you mean exactly?

Lord Vanity: It means, I have been looking for a suitable wife, one that is befitting to a gentleman like myself, one that is good looking, like-minded and intelligent to suit. *(Drops to one knee.)*

106

Let us join together our fortunes and be together as one. Daphne, my dear, will you marry me?

Lady Muck: Yes, of course she will, Lord Vanity.

Daphne: But mother?

Lady Muck: Oh, that's wonderful news, what a beautiful couple you are.

Lord Vanity: Yes, I rather thought so myself. *(Being rather smug and raising an eyebrow.)*

Enter Sir Ivan to loud boos from the audience.

Sir Ivan: What's all this about a marriage, Lord Vanity?

Lady Muck: Get out of my house at once, Sir Ivan, Lord Vanity and Daphne are both madly in love with each other and are now to be man and wife.

Daphne: Why are you here anyway, Sir Ivan?

Lord Vanity: Yes, get out of here at once you, cad,

Sir Ivan: Not so fast, Vanity, I believe a rather large debt is outstanding to me. Your gambling debts are compounding rather fast, haha, it totals your entire estate.

Lady Muck: Is this true, Lord Vanity, do you really owe, Sir Ivan, all that money?

Sir Ivan: I'm afraid it is my dear. I own an online gambling syndicate and Vanity just can't resist tapping his phone screen to make a bet, if he isn't doing that… he's losing at the card table, rather a pathetic gambler, I'd say. He owes me lock, stock and barrel. Ha, haha.

Daphne: But that means… you wanted to marry me, for my money, Lord Vanity?

Lord Vanity: Ah, well my darling, I was having a run of bad luck. It would give me chance to win it back from, Sir Ivan and we could then split the winnings. What do you say?

Daphne: I would never marry you, Lord Vanity, you are a hopeless gambling addict, get out of our house at once.

Lady Muck: Yes you, cad, get out at once. Have my daughter's dowry indeed. You have no more money than… Gordon our gardener.

Lord Vanity: But I love you, Daphne.

All: Out! *He leaves.*

Daphne: And you, Sir Ivan, out!

Sir Ivan: Not so hasty my dear, did I ever mention to you that I am a very, eligible bachelor and… very solvent?

Lady Muck: You are?

Sir Ivan: Yes, my lovely. With my offshore tax haven, I'm worth a fortune. Marry me delightful, Daphne and I will make you a very rich woman.

Daphne: I will never marry you, Sir Ivan.

Lady Muck: Oh, don't be too hasty my dear, every cloud has a silver lining.

Daphne: I would rather die first, Sir Ivan, than marry you.

108

Sir Ivan: Really my dear, then I'm afraid you will… die. *(She screams as he grabs her by the hand to boos from the audience. At this point, Gordon wakes up from his concussion.)*

Gordon: Lady Muck, what has happened to young, Miss Daphne?

Lady Muck: Oh my goodness, Gordon… Daphne has been kidnapped by that bounder, Sir Ivan.

Gordon: But why my lady?

Lady Muck: Because she will not marry him… even though he's got all that money!

Gordon: I'll get after him at once your, Ladyship.
The next sequence is in full melodramatic style with Gordon following Sir Ivan and Daphne in slow motion. The rest of the group make a pier by the seaside. Daphne is tied to a pier post.

Sir Ivan: Well, well… my beauty, I hope you have had time to consider consenting to be my lovely wife? As you can see, you are tied to the post and the sea is rising…very fast.

Daphne: Untie me at once, Sir Ivan.

Sir Ivan: Just say the word… Yes!

Daphne: You are a bounder, Sir Ivan.

Sir Ivan: Yes… ha, ha, ha. And a very rich one.

Daphne: You are also a cad and a vagabond.

Sir Ivan: Is this because you love that other blighter, Lord Vanity, you know the one with no money?

109

Daphne: I would never marry you or him for all the money in the world. Let me go at once, Sir Ivan.

Sir Ivan: If I can't have you, no one will have you, my dear. Hahaha.

Daphne: Let me go you, Brute.

Sir Ivan: Goodbye my dear, Daphne, the water is rising and within minutes you will be gone… forever.

Daphne: Help, help me please, somebody save me.

Gordon comes from behind the pier as the pair meet centre stage. Loud cheers from the audience.

Gordon: Sir Ivan, you are no gentleman, Sir. Untie, Miss Daphne, at once.

Sir Ivan: Or what?

Gordon: Or I'll get very mad with you.

Sir Ivan: What are you going to do, beat me to death with a bunch of flowers?

They pretend to circle one another as though ready to do combat.

Gordon: Look out, Sir Ivan… behind you.

Sir Ivan turns around and stands on Gordon's rake, he is knocked out cold.

Daphne: Help, help, save me, Gordon, the tide is rising and is nearly covering my mouth.

Gordon: I must save the beautiful mistress, I'm coming to save you, Miss Daphne.

110

Mistress Daphne is saved in the nick of time as Gordon unties her from the pier post.

Daphne: Thank you, Gordon, you have saved me from the evil, Sir Ivan and the perils of the rising sea, how could I ever repay you?

Gordon: Miss Daphne, as I give the life to your flowers in your garden, I would give my life to you.

Daphne: I've always loved your commitment to my garden, Gordon, and to me. I've always loved you.

Gordon drops to one knee.

Gordon: Miss Daphne, I could ask for nothing more than your hand in marriage.

Daphne: Three proposals in one day, well… third time lucky!

~

Sir Ivan's Monologue

Sir Ivan is grooming himself in the mirror.

Yes, rather a good night at the old card table. People say gambling is a mug's game. Well, they certainly don't come a bigger mug than that Mumble Mumper, Lord Vanity. He clearly doesn't know when to stop and clearly doesn't know.... that I was cheating! Ha, ha, ha. Oh, I dare say he was a trifle distracted by that mirror behind me. The fool, thinking he could get a reflection of my cards in it. He spent more time admiring his own reflection, too occupied to realise I'd switched the card deck, ha, ha, ha. Alas, Vanity, couldn't stop talking about himself and when the McFluffer told me he had an eye for Lady Daphne, well, I had a little snigger at that one you might say. Imagine her being betrothed to him, who talks of nothing but himself all night, even as his money and estate drained into my hands... through his helpless addiction to gambling. Mmmm, methinks it might be a good idea to pay Lady Daphne a visit tomorrow. Flabberdyegaz, what a wonderful idea. I could do with a little wifey... Yes, she could save on my washing and cleaning bills. By jingo, that's a cunning plan, even if I say so myself.

~

Tasks

Speaking and listening

Melodrama was a popular form of drama in the mid-19th Century with highly over-the-top acting and very stereotypical male characters playing heroes and villains. Females were often portrayed as weak, vulnerable women in distress. **Task 1:** As a class, discuss modern-day melodrama with stereotypical stock characters role's reversed, i.e., strong-minded females who save the men. Think about, Charlie's Angels, Wonder Woman, Lara Croft. **Task 2:** In pairs, using a selection of cartoon captions on a sheet of paper, structure the plot in a continuous linear order to create your own story. **Task 3:** Finally, create groups and rehearse to a performance using strong melodramatic gestures and speech.

Reading

In pairs, discuss Sir Ivan. How would you describe him, his personality, his speech and the language he uses? **Task 1:** Create a wanted poster of Sir Ivan, adding characteristics of him to the sheet and colour all illustrations. **Task 2:** Consider his position as owning a gambling syndicate and how he abuses his position with gambling addicts. Add quotes from Sir Ivan to the poster to enhance this point.

Writing

Melodrama is an old-fashioned style of acting with generally stereotypical plot lines. **Task 1:** Make a list of the pros and cons of melodrama. **Task 2:** Write an article about how you could overcome stereotyping in modern-day melodrama through gender role swapping? Think back again to how women play action heroes. How do they compare with the weak women usually portrayed in old films or plays?

Alternatively, **Task 3:** Write a short story about a teenager who gets drawn into gambling. How could this happen and how could they get addicted to gambling? Think about how young people are encouraged to gamble through computer games and purchasing bonus contents for games. Think about advertising and high-profile personalities encouraging people to gamble.

Extension Task 1: Gambling can be highly addictive and excessive gambling can lead to financial, relationship and mental health problems. Look at the consequences-
https://www.youtube.com/watch?v=IHYaGAQogaw

Extension Task 2: Melodrama is a highly creative style of acting with exaggerated actions and emotions, Research melodrama in more depth.
https://www.elephantmelodrama.com/elephant-melodrama-blog/the-history-and-legacy-of-melodrama

12. You can Count on It.

Characters
Mum/Dad
Teen

Characters' names can be switched on gender. Take your pick, just remember to change the pronouns.

Scene: *Staging of the actor's choice.*

Teen: First days of summer – hanging out with my friends

Mum: But who are these friends – where will it end?

Teen: New friends, old friends – at the street corner.

Mum: Don't be home late – my trust in you, I've warned you.

Teen: On the road end – in the park, in the town.

Mum: Don't think I know – where this could end.

Teen: Kicking through the cut grass – it'll never get dark.

Mum: Be back before dusk – or you know you'll hear my bark.

Teen: Phone volume high – batteries running low.

Mum: I'm not bothered what you play – just keep it on the go.

Teen: Breaking voices singing – a tune from long ago.

115

Mum: You know that I know best – I've always told you so.

Teen: Streaming live music – dancing on the paves.

Mum: Remember what I said to you – or else I'll make some waves.

Teen: A spring in my step – I'm dressing to impress.

Mum: The jeans I bought you – a reward for your good tidiness.

Teen: Time is spinning – it's out of control.

Mum: Let me know where you are – there's always a phone.

Teen: Sun is fast dimming – ahead, a darkness glows.

Mum: Just don't leave me – feeling worried here at home.

Teen: Friends start thinning – time to say, 'Good night.'

Mum: I'm sitting here thinking – all is not right.

Teen: I should be heading home now – I know It's far to go.

Mum: Just make sure – you're never on your own.

Teen: The night was so young – and now it's getting old.

Mum: My trust is running thin – the pain is taking hold.

Teen: Cell batteries flat – perhaps she'll smell a rat.

Mum: Voice mail repeats – I feel I've been deceived.

Teen: I'll get on a bus – then they'll be no fuss.

Mum: Here's a note I have spare – it will keep you in good care.

Teen: But the money wasn't tight – now it doesn't add up to the light.

Mum: It's not for snacks and drinks – it's for when you need it, right.

Teen: Walking into the night – stride away to the dusk.

Mum: Don't set out on foot – you promised me thus.

Teen: A taxi, a taxi – a taxi if I must.

Mum: In case of emergencies – you know what we discussed.

Teen: But mum would go spare – and what if she's bust?

Mum: Please just be careful – this is bigger than both of us.

Teen: She'll be worried now – I will have to explain.

Mum: But she gave me her word – she said this to be heard.

Teen: She might be in some pain – maybe she'll forgive?

Mum: My footsteps repeated – I'm on the phone again.

Teen: I just forgot the time – or maybe she won't mind?

Mum: Her friends are all home now – I'm going out of my mind.

Teen: The road is getting quieter – street lights burning dim.

Mum: My heart is breaking fast – I can feel it within.

Teen: A shortcut to my front door – to face the wrath within.

Mum: Just come home safe – wherever you have been.

Teen: A savour to the rescue? – or trouble from within?

Mum: Remember what I told you – never get in.

Teen: The car is slowing down – red brake lights fill the night.

Mum: I'm feeling dread and anguish – pacing out, not right.

Teen: A window slides slowly down – a shadow within.

Mum: Don't get too close – they'll drag you within.

Teen: 'It's late,' he says. – 'Are you all alone?'

Mum: You wish right then – you had your phone.

Teen: As fast as he appeared – I run and run and run-on home.

Mum: Keep in the light – you made it right, at last, you made it home.

Teen: I know I didn't listen mum – I'll think before I roam.

Mum: My anger turns to happiness – I know now you're safe at home.

Teen: I got away this time around – just thinking of myself.

Mum: And now I know – I'll sleep assured that you are safe and sound.

Teen: In future, I'll let you know – I won't let you down.

118

Mum: To keep in touch – to hear your words, it really isn't that much.

Teen: When I give my word – I will mean what I say.

Mum: A lesson learned – hard as it may.

Teen: To be honest – to you, as long is the day.

~

Teen's Monologue

Teen is reading a letter they have written to their parent/carer.

These thoughts of mine – for all my wrongs.
Are from the heart – to put things right.
I let you down – my fault alone.
Promises given – a shadow alone.
And you at home – left dialling my phone.
I didn't think – when time was a blink.
I promised the earth – and now it's made me think.
To see you upset – is all my fault.
The metre you gave – to the miles I took.
Grounded for months – no doubt bad luck.
I know it's coming – I'll pay my dues.
Pacing the floor – on a carpet worn.
Just hoping and praying – I will open the door.
A parent's trust – after all, is a must.
Sat up for hours – felt waiting in vain.
The desperation you faced – are the lines on this page.

~

Tasks

Speaking and Listening
Discuss the dangers that are presented to teenagers now on social media, whether out of the house or in the home. What do you need to look out for? **Task 1**: Create your own rap, either individually or in pairs, reflecting your views on teenage dangers through social media. It must be a minimum of 10 lines. **Task 2:** Perform it in pairs or as a group to the rest of the class.

Reading
Read the play out loud two or three times. Are there sounds in the language that you could do something with, for example, sound effects that you could add in parts? **Task 1:** Make notes of the effects that could accompany the poem, mark images, places and people who are in the poem. **Task 2:** The 'Teen's Monologue' starts with 'These thoughts of mine are from the heart': write this down on separate lines a minimum of 5 times, now complete each line with biographical details about yourself and turn it into your poem.

Writing
Look at a selection of safety advice leaflets, either online or printed. **Task 1:** How is emotive language used to create an impact on an audience? **Task 2:** Devise a leaflet that encourages young people to be safe and aware when out of their home: What dangers might they look for? Where could these dangers be? Who might they be wary of? How can you be 'smartphone savvy?'

Extension Task
Social media is becoming a fixture of our lives, providing huge benefits but, if used unwisely, causing harm.
Check our social media 'Do's and Don'ts'.
https://www.youtube.com/watch?v=ottnH427Fr8

13. Disconnected Connections

Characters

Mrs/Mr Ellis – Jordan's teacher

Mr./Mrs Rosewell – Jordan's parent
Characters' names can be switched on gender. Take your pick, just remember to change the pronouns.

Scene: *A school office.*

Mrs Ellis: Thank you for coming into school, Mr Rosewell, please take a seat.

Mr Rosewell: Yes, I will… but I must say, I'm not happy about this, my wife and I both work full-time and we are very busy.

Mrs Ellis: Yes, it's an inconvenience for both of us, so let's hope this is a one-off.

Mr Rosewell: I mean, asking me to come to school, just because my son has had his phone confiscated in your lesson. Don't you think it's a bit over the top?

Mrs Ellis: There was a bit more to it than that, Mr Rosewell.

Mr Rosewell: Well, that's what he told me, you shouted at him for using it in the lesson and sent him out of the classroom.

Mrs Ellis: What you have been told is one version of events, Mr Rosewell, the reality is a bit different.

Mr Rosewell: He told me he was doing some research on, 'google' he was showing initiative as far as I'm concerned!

Mrs Ellis: He was doing a mock exam… if it was the real thing, he would be suspended, and the exam disqualified.

Mr Rosewell: But he was taking responsibility for finding the answers from what you've just said.

Mrs Ellis: Mr Rosewell, you seem to be encouraging, Jordan's sense of wrong over right. To deserve everything without earning it. Jordan's phone alerts sounded off, disrupting the class and the exam, furthermore, he challenged me on the use of it. His attitude was rude, leaving me no choice but to send him outside the class. I gave him lunchtime detention and I have to say his attitude still did not change. I wasn't very happy with him, to say the least.

Mr Rosewell: I'm sure he wasn't very happy himself, it's not what he would want.

Mrs Ellis: It's not what he wants, Mr Rosewell, it's what he needs. I am very concerned about how difficult Jordan finds it to communicate and accept even basic failings.

Mr Rosewell: Well, he likes his phone, it keeps him stimulated, provides technical information that he may need, maybe he was just missing that?

Mrs Ellis: I get the impression he's not used to someone saying, 'No' to him?

Mr Rosewell: Not at all… it's just that he hates that word.

Mrs Ellis: Yes and No are the fundamentals of life. He disrupted a test for the rest of the class, a test that was necessary for preparing him for his end of year exams. His attitude is causing me concern, also with his behaviour. Is that a concern to you, Mr Rosewell?

Mr Rosewell: Er, yes, I, er… suppose so.

123

Mrs Ellis: Does he spend a lot of time on his phone?

Mr Rosewell: Oh yes, he's always glued to those screens but they're educational, aren't they?

Mrs Ellis: Screens?

Mr Rosewell: Well, yes. He has his computer and his smartphone, oh… and his, iPad, everything to help him at school.

Mrs Ellis: It depends on what he's using them for, not if he's just playing games on them, is he?

Mr Rosewell: Er… I don't know, I er… haven't checked, he er... has a games consul, but that's just for games, isn't it?

Mrs Ellis: Do you restrict his use of screen time in the evening?

Mr Rosewell: Er… No.

Mrs Ellis: Why not?

Mr Rosewell: That would really get him… well, angry. We have enough trouble with him sorting his bedroom out or hanging his clothes upon a night, or getting his kit packed for school the next day. So, we, er.

Mrs Ellis: Let him… do what he wants? Do you mind me asking but who packs his kit for school?

Mr Rosewell: That would be his mother, we're rushing around first thing in the morning. It just makes things easier if she picks it up. I can then put it in the car for him, it's so much quicker all around. To be honest Mrs Ellis… actually, I am a bit worried about, Jordan, he's always tired and very augmentative.

Mrs Ellis: Yes, he sounds like he has a sedentary lifestyle.

124

Mr Rosewell: I wish he would do a bit more around the house, you know like clearing the kitchen table, washing up, or maybe take the dog out for a walk. But everything's an argument with him and it's just not worth the disturbance in the house, so we let him… work on technology through his phone time. I suppose it always fills a space; he's never bored… I think. I mean, keeping busy is a good thing isn't it, learning new things through technology?

Mrs Ellis: I'm not sure if instant gratification through endless stimulation on-screen time is the answer, Mr Rosewell, boring moments are important, providing you have the tools to master it. Boredom is the moment when creativity can begin, it can be a moment to train the brain to learn how to connect and socialise with others. Also, not be socially isolated through technology. I mean, does he communicate with you, interact with his family?

Mr Rosewell: Er… no not really, you know how it is with teenagers? Lucky if you get a grunt, never mind a please or a thank you. *Silence… Pause.*
To tell the truth, Mrs Ellis, I'm really worried about him, his behaviour and his attitude, but I just don't know what to do, neither does my wife… do you?

Mrs Ellis: *(Gently.)* Would you like my advice?

Mr Rosewell: Yes… I really would.

Mrs Ellis: I think you have to get back to basics Mr Rosewell, your teenage son is ruling his and your world, you're the 'Pilot of the Ship' so consider these: setting limits, don't be afraid to say, 'No' to digital distractions at night. Maybe enjoy dinner together without smartphones, play board games, connect as a family. I think it's the world of today that we miss most of all… Perhaps it's just playing together, talking together, whatever. I hope this will help Mr Rosewell.

125

Mr Rosewell: In any particular order?

~

Mr Rosewell's Monologue

*Mr Rosewell is reflecting on his visit to Jordan's Head of Year. Characters'
names can be switched on gender. Take your pick, just remember to change the
pronouns.*

There are two sides to each story and I've just heard a very
different one from, Mrs Ellis. As a father, am I at fault here or…?
I guess it's both of us. I know deep down I've been living in
denial, not taking my share of responsibility, Mrs Ellis, is certainly
clear about that. I thought technology might help, you know, with
research for lessons but disrupting lessons with phone alerts in a
test and then challenging the teacher… I mean, this attitude and
behaviour has got to stop. I think we need to bring in restrictions
before bedtime on phone use, it's disrupting sleep patterns and we
get all the bad moods first thing in the morning. And another
thing, I'm not packing or carrying bags to school, it's walking to
school from now on, and exercise will break this lazy cycle. You
know, the more I think about it, the more we need to
communicate. We don't even talk as a family, always engaged on
a phone screen… I mean we're becoming disconnected… do you
not agree…? I mean what do you think…? *(He reacts to an imaginary
Mrs Rosewell who turns her attention from her phone and stares back at him.)*
Please, would you mind putting your phone down, just for a
minute… you're my wife and, if we can't agree on this, we've got
no chance with our son, Jordan.

~

Tasks

Speaking and listening.

Discuss together, a time when the Rosewell family were happier and connected with one and other on a family outing. **Task 1**: Imagine you are one of the Rosewell family, pick any character. Write a diary of the family outing and consider what were the highs and lows of the day? Who was with them, what did they do, where did they go, when was it? **Task 2:** Using freeze frames at important points in the diary, allow each scene to come to life for one minute. This could allow the actors to multi-role at various points within the story. **Task 3:** Create a present-day presentation of the family. Demonstrate the contrast between them connecting when they were happier in the past to the disconnected family in the present.

Reading

Reread the story of the incident in the class and the mock exam. **Task 1:** On a sheet of paper, split it in half with two lists. One on the benefits of smart technology and the other on the negative impact they have. Consider the balance of benefits and negatives.

Writing

Task 1: Research how letters to problem pages are set out and then write a letter from Mr Roswell to an agony aunt/uncle asking for advice on how to cope with Jordan's problems. Then write the response as it might appear in a newspaper's agony column.

Extension Task

Procrastination is attention switching and postponing the work that you have to do. An example might be, whilst doing your homework, checking your phone and then carrying on distracted with that device instead of what you have to do. **Task 1:** Research how you can change this behaviour.

https://www.youtube.com/watch?v=pjgngyfxIzM

14. Body Image

Characters
Bev - Young Teen
Nat - Young Teen
Harley - Young Teen
Brad - Young Teen

Scene 1: Saturday in town. The girls are talking about themselves and how they compare to celebrities on their phones.

Bev: You've got to admit it, G, she is so cool, just look at how many followers she's got.

Nat: She looks amazing, I wonder if she ever looks at her followers?

Bev: Probably, I mean, wouldn't it be great if she replied to one of our posts?

Nat: Get real, Bev, she lives in a mansion in, LA. I don't think she'll be looking at us.

Bev: Every time I see that new video of her, she looks so peng.

Nat: And she's only 17. Who do you have to know to be famous at such a young age?

Bev: It's not about who you know, Nat, it's about talent... she won the Wow Factor at 14. Of course, being good looking helps. I mean, I just can't get over her hair, it's so shiny and long.

Nat: Do you think it's real?

130

Bev: Of course it is, haven't you seen her advertising that conditioner. It would fall off in the shower if it wasn't. And what about those nails, they're sick. I'm gonna get some of those.

Nat: You mean, when you've got some money from your mum, you will.

Bev: Oh, yeah, she'll give in and I'll be down at the nail shop, they've even got diamonds on them.

Nat: Knowing, April Grenola, they'll be real diamonds. Trouble is, even fake nails are banned at school.

Bev: That's such a stupid rule.

Nat: They say it damages your nail beds when we're growing up.

Bev: Who ever thought of that is damaged! I just so wish I could be her, the eyes, the make-up, the way she holds that cigarette.

Nat: Do you believe she only smokes to keep her weight down?

Bev: Who cares, she certainly looks good on them, Look at that pose, I'd love to be able to pout like that. *(Bev imitates this into her phone screen.)*

Nat: Ah but look at that Bikini… I'd never wear one of those, I'd be too embarrassed, I'd never match up to her.

Bev: Why not?

Nat: I'm too fat.

Bev: Have you thought of dieting?

Nat: Oh, thanks a lot, Bev, I just couldn't be seen in one that's all, even on holiday. It's alright for you, you've got the perfect figure,

131

the perfect face. You even look like, April Grenola.

Bev: Yeah, I know, a lot of people say I do. But I have to work on it, Nat, I skipped lunch every day last week.

Nat: Really?

Bev: Yeah, really, if you want to get into those super skinny jeans, you've got to work on it, girl.

Nat: Erm, but I really love my lunch.

Bev: So did I, Nat, but a moment on the lips... a lifetime on the hips and you've got?

Both: Weight!

Bev: Come on, let's take a selfie and send it to April, maybe she might reply.

Nat: Oh, can it wait, my hair's a mess and you've curled yours.

Bev: I know it looks great, doesn't it? Anyway, put this hat on *(Holds her phone, takes selfie and posts the picture.)* 'BFF luv u April. Lol.' Even if she doesn't respond, let's see how many likes I get?

Nat: Don't you mean, what 'we' get, Bev?

Bev: Yeah, Yeah, Don't look now G but guess who I've just clocked?

They both turn around and look and freeze as stage left enters Brad and Harley.

Brad: Hey, Harley, isn't that?

Harley: Yeah, Bev and Nat ... just play it cool.

132

Brad: Sure, whatever you say. What are you pointing at?

Harley: Just pretend we're looking at something across the road, I'll hold my chin.

Brad: Er, yeah, oh I get it, like one of those male models!

Harley: You've got it in one, *(He puts on his sunglasses.)*

Brad: Harley, it looks like it's gonna rain, and what you doing unbuttoning the front of your shirt? You'll freeze to death?

Harley: I haven't spent six months on that rowing machine for nothing.

Brad: It must have sunk.

Harley: Eh, you what? Haven't you seen a sculptured chest before, if it's good enough for, Ronaldo it's good enough for Bev and Nat.

Brad: I didn't realise you were so tanned as well, Harley?

Harley: Bit of fake tan, nicked it off mum. No point in having the physique of Ronaldo if you haven't got the colour to match.

Brad: Or the talent?

Harley: Watch it, you. Anyway, watch this, *(Harley puts his hand under his bicep and pushes out his muscles.)* Are they looking?

Brad: I think so, but the one that looks like, April Grenola is blowing kisses into her phone.

Harley: Hmmm, Maybe she has a boyfriend?

133

Brad: Or maybe she's more interested in herself? Why don't you check her profile?

Harley: Good idea, Brad, not just a hat rack *(Points to Brad's head.)* She's very popular, nearly as many likes as me.

Brad: Let's ask them what they're up to on her post? Her mate's cute, she looks well fit.

Harley: Watch this *(He types.)* 'Looking fit… and hey, you don't look 2 bad yourself. lol.'

Stage right.

Bev: *(Reading the text.)* 'Looking fit… and hey, you don't look 2 bad yourself. lol.'

Nat: I think he knows that! What have they said about me? I'm in the photo as well you know.

Bev: Nothing.

Nat: Nothing?

Bev: Just be grateful they haven't mentioned your, Vampire teeth.

Nat: It's not my fault I wear a brace, it's only for two more years, and I'm trying to cover it.

Bev: I know, but when your hands are over your mouth, I can't always hear what you say.

Nat: I didn't think you listened anyway.

Bev: Look, just be normal, as normal as you can be, I don't want to miss out on, Harley.

134

Nat: That's not a nice thing to say, Bev.

Bev: I'm just being honest.

Nat: It's your honesty that bothers me.

Bev: Well, let's type up this message or I'll lose the best-looking guy in our year. We'll make a great couple, me and Harley, we'll be like a celebrity couple.

Nat: Give me strength.

Bev: *(Typing.)* 'What u up 2?'

Stage right.

Harley: *(Typing.)* 'Fancy going to the fair?

Stage left.

Bev: *(Types.)* 'Ok, the fair, lol'.

Nat: Look they're coming over,

They meet centre stage.

All: THE FAIR.

Harley: So, where do you fancy going first?

Nat: Look, there're some footballs and nets over there, hit the target and we could win a prize.

Brad: Sounds mint, I'll bet I can hit it first. Come on then let's go.

Bev and Harley: Are you kidding?

Bev: I am not getting these white trousers dirty, it's alright for you, you're in scruffy jeans, Nat.

Harley: I am not kicking a ball in these boots, they cost me a packet. You're in trainers, Brad.

Nat: OK, how about the 'Big Dipper', it looks sick.

Brad: It'll be a scream.

Bev and Harley: Are you kidding?

Bev: My hair will look like I've been electrocuted if I went on that, you don't have to worry about that with your hair?

Nat: What's that supposed to mean?

Bev: I'm just saying… We'd all look a bit stupid doing those things.

Harley: Bev's right, If I sat in that contraption with these skinny jeans, I wouldn't be able to walk… or talk for a week!

Brad: Well, what do you fancy doing… please?

Bev: We could stand here and watch.

Harley: Yeah, that sounds a good idea, stand here and watch… what's going on.

Nat: You mean, stand here and let other people watch you?

Brad: Playing with your phones comparing each other.

Nat: Oh come on, Brad, let's go, I've had enough of this.

Brad: Bouncy Castle?

136

Nat: Why not. *(They run stage right to the Bouncy Castle, take off their shoes and start bouncing around.)*

Harley: They are so immature. *(Harley stretches his arms and brings it down on Bev's shoulder, he turns into her.)*

Bev: Ahhh, you've got your shirt button caught in my earring!

Harley: Oh… so sorry Bev *(Trying to unclip it.)*

Bev: Ahhh… You've spiked me in the eye with your hair, what you gelled it with… fibreglass?

On the Bouncy Castle.

Brad: Why do you keep your hand over your mouth, you've got a lovely smile.

Nat: What, even with this? *(She points to her brace.)*

Brad: Yeah, even with that. *(Smiling.)*

Nat: So, do you want 'jazz hands' from now on? *(Waving her hands in the air.)*

Brad: Yeah, all the time, for me.

Nat: Ok, just this once, for you.

Brad and Nat: *(Both take a natural pose as Nat takes the selfie.)* 'Jazz hands…lol X'

Nat: I'm gonna send that to, April Grenola… and let her know what she's missing.

Stood stage left.

Bev: Look, it was your idea to come to the fair.

Harley: Well, it's not my fault it's raining, is it?

Bev: Well, it's not my fault my heels are sinking into the mud, my curly hair is frizzing and my teeth are sticking together.

Harley: You asked for the toffee apple, I wouldn't mind you hardly touched it and it cost me a packet, so don't blame… *(He is stopped in mid-sentence by Bev as her phone pings.)*

Bev: Look, it's a photo of, Nat and Brad, on the Bouncy Castle, 'Jazz hands lol X'.

Harley: I don't believe it… April Grenola's responded to it!

Bev: The… April Grenola… No way?

Harley: Yes way. Look what it says, 'Youth I do adore thee.'… BFF April Grenola X'

Bev: I don't get it, why of all people would, April, reply to them?

Harley: Yeah… and of all the things, why would she say… that?

~

Bev's Monologue

Bev is in her bathroom getting herself ready to go out.

Nat is really getting on my nerves, just because she and Brad are getting on so well. I mean who does she think she is? I'm number one in this group and just because it didn't work out with, Harley, well that's not my fault… at all. *(She starts to take a selfie.)* I know I'd look a bit better if I lost another pound… maybe around my hips, perhaps I'd feel better? Just look at, April's waist, it's incredible. Mind you, she's probably got her own personal trainer knowing her, whilst I have to do it all the hard way. *(She fanatically starts doing sit-ups.)* I still don't look right, what is it? Oh, this is all, April's, fault and to top it all, mums cooking a big dinner tonight. I've tried to get out of it but I can't, it will ruin my diet. Oh well, I guess I am actually quite hungry, I don't know why? Anyway, I've no choice in the matter now, I'll just have to eat it. The only problem is, when the food arrives, I don't feel like it. It's like I start to feel it's all wrong and then mum starts looking at me, which makes it worse and I start pushing the food around the plate. Anyway, I can always make my excuses and bring it back up in the toilet, she'll never know. Oh, I just wish my mum would leave me alone, she's really doing my head in. I just can't see what the problem is.

~

Tasks

Speaking and listening
Discuss what might be going through each character's mind, what feelings and emotions are they experiencing? How might their body image be affected by online comparisons? Why is health more important than trending on social media? **Task 1:** Discuss and create a 'Reality TV Show' where the guests are Bev and Nat, or Brad and Harley reflecting on their experiences together and what they think about the date and current pressure on young people using social media.

Reading
Perceptions, **Task 1:** Using clues in the play's storyline, make a list of the good and bad ways that social media has affected the characters' behaviour. How could you overcome the bad effects without stopping social media altogether?

Writing
Task 1: Write an essay explaining how we can feel comfortable and confident in who we are, without needing to conform to social media influences about how we look and act. This can be done in three sections: How can we feel confident in ourselves? How does the media influence our decisions? Finally, a conclusion on the balance of your understanding of conformity.

Extension Task
Draw a basic costume figure on a blank piece of paper. Design a suitable costume for a character of your choice. Using arrows, annotate the design, referring to the period the play is set and the choice of garments, colours, styles, etc. Also, consider elements of hair and makeup that would add emphasis to the character.

15. The Photograph Album

Physical Theatre is using your body to create shapes, objects, props and letters. It is used frequently in modern theatre because it is inexpensive and the actor and the audience have to use more imagination to engage with the performance.

<u>Characters</u>
Nicki/Nicky
Actor 1 - Stevie/Steve
Actor 2 - Mr/ Mrs Brown.
Actor 3 - Uncle John/ Auntie Janet
Characters' names can be switched on gender. Take your pick, just remember to change the pronouns.

Scene 1*: Actors 1 & 2 create the top and bottom of the bed. Actor 3 creates the alarm clock for Nicki, who is fast asleep. She is awoken by the alarm clock and sits up in bed facing and addressing the audience.*

Nicki: Saturday, don't you just love Saturdays? No registration, no lessons, no school, no homework… well just a bit, but it can wait till tomorrow afternoon, because today I'm chilling and… first things first, let's have that TV on. *(She mimes an imaginary remote.)*

Actors 1,2, & 3 create a TV screen, out of it they come to life, speaking and acting as a current TV show. When this is finished Nicki addresses the audience.

Nicki: Today I'm meeting my best friend, Stevie, in town. We've both got vouchers and we're going to do some serious shopping. But hang on, all this talking is going to make me late, I've got to get showered and changed.

The next scene is made by actors 1.2.& 3 who create a working shower cubicle, with temperature dials and running water. This is done with, Nicki, singing one of the current songs of the day in the shower, the shower can join in with the chorus.

Nicki: Don't you just love to sing in the shower?

Actors: 2&3 create a sink with actor 1 creating a mirror for Nicki to brush her teeth and sort hair/makeup out. Nicki talks into a mirror.

Nicki: We didn't always get along, Stevie and me, we first met in the school canteen cueing for food. *(The mirror comes alive now as actor 1 becomes Stevie to create a flashback of their first meeting.)*

Stevie: Excuse me, you've just pushed in

Nicki: No, I haven't, Simon was keeping my place for me.

Stevie: I don't think so, where's Simon?

Nicki: He's just gone to the toilet; I'm keeping his place till he gets back.

Stevie: You're making it up.

Nicki: Are you calling me a liar? *(Pushes Stevie.)*

Stevie: Who do you think you're pushing?

Nicki: And then the teacher came and sent us both to the 'Head of Year'

Actors 1,2, & 3 now make a wardrobe with sliding/opening doors. As they open Actor 1 is on the rail as a garment. Nicki is looking at the garment in the wardrobe mirror.

142

Nicki: It was my fault and I knew I'd pushed in; I also knew I was in big trouble.

Actor 2 steps out and becomes Mrs Brown, Head of Year.

Mrs Brown: Right, I've heard you started this, Nicki.

Nicki: I'm sorry miss, It was...

Stevie: *(Actor 1 steps out.)* Er, it wasn't just her, Miss, we were both to blame.

Nicki: I was shocked, I knew it was my fault and I was ready for the blame, but Stevie took half of the hit for me. I knew then, Stevie was a friend, a friend I could trust. Someone I knew I could talk to… about anything.

Actors 1, 2 and 3 create the staircase in the present time for Nicki to walk down, this is done safely giving an illusion of Nicki walking down the stairs.

Nicki: We talk about school, family, friends, sport, games, phones, boys, girls, but most of all music. We both have a love for songs, singers and bands. We listen to the latest songs through streaming and downloads on our phones.

Actors 2 & 3 create the breakfast table for Nicki and Stevie to sit on either side. They create a toaster, teapot and cup for her to eat and drink. Nicki addresses the audience again.

Nikki: Guess what, Stevie's got her for her birthday?
Actor 1 becomes Stevie.

Stevie: My, Aunt Janet, gave me her old turntable, also called a record player, for those that need educating!   It's brilliant ... but I've got no records, no vinyl!

143

Nicki: So today, we are going to buy our first vinyl with our hard-earned spends.

Stevie: And we are going to listen to it, track by track, song by song… on a record player.

Actors all create the front of a house with a front door, Nicki steps out through it, turns and locks it and waits for a bus.

Nicki: I've also got a birthday surprise in store for, Stevie.

Stevie: Tell me, what is it?

Nicki: It wouldn't be a surprise then, would it? You'll have to wait.

Stevie: I hate waiting for surprises!

Actors 2&3 create a bus, the doors open and Stevie is standing up on the bus waiting for Nicki. The pair give the illusion they are travelling on the bus.

Nicki: At first, I thought what's the point in buying vinyl records?

Stevie: And then we thought about the artwork on the sleeve, the notes on the inside.

Nicki: Also, not forgetting … we will actually own it.

They arrive at an imaginary building that houses the music store, which has rotating doors in the entrance. This is created by the actor 2&3 for Nicki and Stevie.
This morphs into a lift door by actors 2 & 3. It takes them to the second floor, and the sound of the lift is made by both actors. Stevie and Nicki speak to the audience.

Stevie: My, Uncle John, told me that he threw all his vinyl away.

144

Uncle John: *(Actor 2 steps out.)* I can't believe my stupidity; I just didn't think vinyl records would ever come back and they were all piled up in the garage. We moved to a new house and I gave them away, now it's certainly music to somebody's wallet!

Nicki: My, Auntie Janet, said:

Auntie Janet: *(Actor 3 steps out.)* Oh, Nicki, I can still remember the first record I ever bought, bringing it back home and playing it till I wore the grooves out.

Nicki: I think she said it was by a Starman…

Auntie Janet: 'Let the children boogie.'

Stevie: Why not?

Auntie Janet: Nicki, my vinyl is like a photograph album of my life, knowing where I come from… to where I'm going now. It helps me from repeating the mistakes of the past… and I should know, I've made a few.

Nicki: Do you think of the past, Stevie? I mean everybody is telling me to plan for the future.

Stevie: Mr Richards, our English teacher, told us to bring the future into the present, so we can deal with it now, so we can plan ahead.

Nicki: He's strange!

Stevie: Past, present and the future.

Nicki: Do you think we'll remember this moment, Stevie, here and now?

Stevie: I don't know let's play the record!

145

Nicki: Ok, but before we do, I have this for you. *(She hands Stevie an imaginary envelope with two tickets in it for her favourite band.)*

Stevie: Nicki, this is amazing... tickets to see our favourite band, 'Landscape.'

Nicki and the actors all create the record player with the group all singing or playing a recording of a song from the present time.

~

Nicki's Monologue

Nicki is talking to Aunt Janet.

Getting this birthday present for Stevie has been easy, well not that easy to get actually… but the idea for the present was easy. That's because I know what Stevie likes and Stevie knows what I like… Which is usually the same thing! Both of us are really into a band called Landscape. They're different you see, they play their own instruments, write their own songs and play like they believe in what they're playing. So, when I found out that tickets were on sale for their gig down at the City Hall, I knew I just had to go. I begged my mum and dad if I could go with Stevie… and they've agreed to it. They said they'll take us there and pick us up at the end. It's just soooo brilliant, isn't it, Aunt Janet? I spent hours online trying to buy them, it wasn't easy I can tell you… but I got them. I downloaded them and printed them off, and now, I'm giving them as a surprise to Stevie, today. I just hope her parents will agree to it. This will be my first gig and I can't wait… Can you remember your first gig, Aunt Janet?

~

Tasks

Speaking and listening

The depictions of the house, bus and record department store are created through imagination and physically constructed using all the actors in the play. These are marking key moments in growing up, developing new interests and friendships that create memorable experiences to look back on. **Task 1:** Give an account of a place you enjoy visiting or a special interest you have. This can be in the form of a written task or a speech to the group. **Task 2:** Using physical theatre and improvisation, rehearse and perform your account.

Reading

Take a closer look at the script and the characters that deliver a direct address to the audience. **Task 1:** Make a list of these characters and write key points about each one, looking specifically at their character motivation? (What do they want to achieve in each line of each scene?) Try and select key lines in the play to demonstrate your points.

Writing

Pupils use their knowledge of an interest that they have, e.g., a particular artist, band, film, football club they enjoy. **Task 1:** Write a magazine review of the experience, using journalistic style to grab the reader's imagination. Below is an example of a music review of Billie Eilish at Glastonbury.

What an entrance, what a start. Power up to full throttle, a mighty roar from a welcoming crowd and what have you got? Billie Eilish, captivating her solid, growing fan base. The set, straight out of a 'Hammer Horror' film with gothic overtures. Its visual menacing overtones with Eilish in panther stalking mode, prowling the proscenium with threat and charisma. She opens up with 'Bad Guy' that hits the right chord with its chest-thumping bass line. The crowd are instantly receptive, moving and bouncing as one, excited to the beat and the dazzling lights flashing across our faces of wonderment.

148

Even parents, adults, security personal are nodding their heads to the grinding beat, losing self-conscious embarrassment, feeling the abandonment of responsibility as her music transports us to another planet, another universe. No idle chat between songs, straight into, 'You should see me in a Crown.' This personal, yet cynical understanding of her status as 'The Real Deal' in an industry of 'Wannabe Fakers.' She throws down her marker-She doesn't say it, but her body language displays it. 'Well, who wants to take me on, who dares to take me on? Billie is here… for the foreseeable future.

Extension Task: Research how to create the perfect magazine article.

https://www.youtube.com/watch?v=CAZB2PSm5UU

16. An English Breakfast

Characters
Characters' names can be switched on gender. Take your pick, just remember to change the pronouns.

Eva/Evan - Teenage student
Kyle/Kylie - Teenage student
Sir/Miss - Teacher

Scene: *Eva and Kylie are standing up in a science lab, working on an experiment.*

Eva: How far is it off morning break?

Kylie: No idea, I haven't got a watch, but I hope it's soon.

Eva: It must be getting close; my stomach's rumbling and it's giving me some pain.

Kylie: Put your hand up and ask to see the school nurse.

Eva: She won't do anything; she'll send me straight back to the lesson with a wet paper towel on my forehead... even if my leg was hanging off.

Kylie: You're not wrong there.

Eva: It's the cook I need, not the nurse. I'm starving.

Kylie: You must have had something for breakfast?

Eva: Sort off, but I was late up and I didn't want to miss my lift to school off mum.

Kylie: Eh..? You only live just round the corner from school!

150

Eva: I'm saving on shoe leather.

Kylie: But you sort of had something for breakfast, what did you have?

Eva: Well, mum gave me some money for a sandwich.

Kylie: That should see you till break.

Eva: Yeah, but I bought a large bag of salt and vinegar crisps and a bar of chocolate instead.

Kylie: At least you've had something this morning, I've had nothing.

Eva: Ah sorry, I forgot… were you at your dad's last night?

Kylie: Yes, every Sunday night.

Eva: I hope you don't think I'm being rotten, but you're more used to not having breakfast before morning break, so it won't affect you… you know… the same as me.

Kylie: You what?

Eva: I'm sorry… I didn't mean it that way, look I know we're friends, you can have the chocolate at break. I still have some left in my bag.

Kylie: Oh, you're too generous, but I'll hold you to that. Look out, the teacher's clocked us. *(They put their heads down pretending to work.)*

Teacher: Kylie, will you cut out the chat and concentrate on the task I've set for you. I can't see a lot of progression in this experiment. This is your first and last warning.

Kylie: Yes Miss… Thanks, Eva. *(A long pause.)*

151

Eva: When this lesson's over, let's put our skates on so we won't be at the back of the canteen queue. I don't want to be fighting for the last stale bacon sandwich.

Kylie: Shhh, button it will you.

Eva: Did you just say butter it?

Kylie: Hah, now you're hearing things.

Eva: If I get any hungrier, I'll be seeing things!

Kylie: Anyway, I've no money.

Eva: I'll sub you some.

Kylie: I'm not borrowing off you again… look out, we've been spotted.

Teacher: That's it, Kylie, you've had your warning. Every time I've looked in your direction you're talking and not doing your work. You're staying behind at break.

Kylie: But, Miss *(looking at Eva for support.)*

Teacher: No buts, you're staying behind through break. Right class, stop what you are doing and copy the homework from the board into your planners… Now put your equipment away, please.

Kylie: *(She turns on Eve.)* Well, aren't you going to say anything? You're the one who hasn't stopped talking and it's me who's getting the DT. We're supposed to be friends… aren't we?

Eva: I really need some food, it sends me a bit hyper when I'm hungry and I'll crack up if I don't get any, I'll get you something, I promise, I owe you.

Kylie: *(Raising voice.)* Don't you think I'm hungry? Some friend you are leaving me here.

Teacher: And you're still talking, Kylie, Right class, have my homework ready for my next lesson. Kylie, stay where you are, the rest, off you go.

Everyone goes including Eva, leaving Kylie fuming.

Teacher: Right, Kylie, why were you talking despite the previous warnings you've had from me?

Kylie: *(Doesn't say anything.)*

Teacher: Well, I hope you're going to answer me or this will run into a lunchtime detention.

Kylie: It's not fair, Miss.

Teacher: It's also not fair disrupting the rest of the class and my lesson.

Kylie: But it's all wrong.

Teacher: What's all wrong, tell me what part of being quiet and focusing on each task do you not understand. What's wrong with that?

Kylie: *(Raising her voice.)* It's just that... It's not right. *(Kylie is close to breaking down.)*

Teacher: Okay, calm down, you're getting upset now, but without telling me, how will I know what's underlying here?

Kylie: But it's just... it's always me, that does without.

Teacher: How do you mean, Kylie, without what? If you don't let me know, how will I understand?

Kylie is silent with her head down and starts to sob. There is a silence as Eva returns to the classroom.

Eva: I think I can explain it, Miss, it's not, Kylie's fault, it's mine, Kylie was telling me to be quiet. I was doing all the talking, well… complaining. I was hungry. *(Kylie looks up)* I'm sorry Miss, I'm sorry, Kylie. I really am.

Teacher: Well, I appreciate your honesty, Eva, if nothing else, but Kylie here has been getting upset. Would you like to tell me what's been going on? *(Kylie remains silent as Eva chips in.)*

Eva: I skipped my breakfast, Miss, as I was running late and it makes me a bit giddy, especially when it's close to morning break.

Teacher: Have you had nothing to eat or drink since you got up?

Eva: Oh, I've had some crisps… and some chocolate.

Teacher: But that's the worst thing you could eat, it will send your metabolism into shock, it could play havoc with your weight in later years. Do you not have cereal? Ideally, porridge is perfect to kick start your day and it's a slow burner to hold off hunger pangs.

Eva: We've got loads of different cereals; it's just I didn't want to miss my lift to school from my mum.

Teacher: Well, get up earlier in the future, Eva, especially if you have to travel far to get to school.

Kylie: She only lives on, Crawford Avenue, Miss. *(Starts to giggle and lighten up.)*

Teacher: But that's just around the corner from school?

154

Eva: It's all uphill, Miss!

Teacher: Good grief, Eva, exercise and a good diet are key to being healthy and a long life, it also helps your concentration, as does water to rehydrate you. I'm sure you must be aware of your lack of focus today. Now I hope you're feeling better, Kylie. *(She is better.)* So, what about you, I hope you've had your breakfast?

Kylie: *(Head down.)* Er no, Miss…

Teacher: Why not?

Kylie: Because I stay with my dad on Sunday nights and there's nothing in… well you know… he's a bit disorganised.

Teacher: So… you've had nothing to eat at all today?

Eva: She never does, Miss, on Monday mornings.

Teacher: You must be hungry, Kylie?

Kylie: I am, miss, I don't get giddy, I just get, annoyed…

Eva: She gets 'Hangry' Miss.

Teacher: I think I would too. Have you got enough money for some food, Kylie?

Kylie: I'm on free school meals, Miss.

Teacher: *(Deep in thought.)* Now, Kylie, does your father have cereal in the house?

Kylie: Yes, Miss, but no milk. He sleeps till late in the morning and… well, I don't like to bother him.

Teacher: *(Deep in thought about Kylie.)* Right, you must mention this

155

to him, so you can have breakfast before you come to school. You are going to have to get organised Sunday night and make sure everything is in place ready for you in the morning. Take some milk from your mums in a small container, just to be certain you have some for the morning. We'll catch up on this again next week. In the meantime, you will need this whilst you wait in the canteen queue. *(She passes Kylie an apple.)*

Kylie: It's alright, Miss.

Teacher: No, it's fine, take it… Go on, off you go.

Kylie: Thank you, Miss. *(She eagerly eats it as she sets off out of the classroom.)* Miss, I always thought it was the other way round, isn't it the pupil who's supposed to bring the apple in for the teacher?

Teacher: *(The teacher laughs and turns to her desk computer.)* At this moment, I'd settle for a coffee… Off you go and don't miss your break.

~

Kylie's Monologue

Characters' names can be switched on gender. Take your pick, just remember to change the pronouns.

I sometimes sub some money from my friend, Eva, she's always loaded. Her mum gives her dinner money to buy what she calls, 'Nourishing food'…but she never bothers with that, she normally spends it on her favourite bar of chocolate. That's at the shop near school. I hate borrowing from her… it leaves me with a feeling of owing somebody something… and that's something I can't pay back. Now it's 'payday'… because, Eva, wants a favour from me and I've got to pay her back. It's sports day and Eva hates sports day. I'm pretty good at the 400m, it doesn't bother me. But Eva hates any running… or any exercise come to think of it. She says it's because she hates wearing her PE kit. She doesn't like people looking at her. She's gonna skip school this afternoon and she wants me to cover for her. Eva's typed a letter… well, forged a letter. It says she has a dental appointment. She wants me to sign it and then… give it to, Miss Jackson in registration… I just hope, I don't get into trouble for it… I'm really scared.

~

Tasks

Speaking and listening

Hot seating gives the actor the chance to develop the character through working in a role, improvising and firming up traits through questioning by fellow actors. **Task 1:** Pick any of one of the three characters, each member of the class must think of a minimum of 5 questions they can ask their peers whilst in the role, and then write them down as a list. The actor, in role, must try to believe and react to how the character would respond in all situations, experimenting with voice, movement and gesture.

Reading

Looking closer at the script again, Eva chooses not to eat healthy food even though she is given money to do so, whilst Kylie has less choice but chooses to eat healthy given the opportunity. **Task 1:** Make a list of five foods that are a healthy option and five which are unhealthy. **Task 2:** Whilst we could spend a lot on food, the cheaper options can often be the ones that we should be eating the most of. From the five healthy examples in your list, explain why each one is healthier for you?

Writing

Descriptive writing. **Task 1:** Create a breakfast menu as an advertisement for a café bar you are opening. Give at least three choices of healthy food and different healthy drinks. Try to use lots of adjectives to entice your customers to buy them.

Extension Task: Research how to sell using adjectives.
https://www.signs.com/sell-the-sizzle/

17. Free Gifts

Characters
Allan - Adult
Liz - Teen girl

Scene: In the front and back of a takeaway food outlet.

Liz: *(Speaking a 'Direct address' to the audience.)* It's nice when someone pays attention to you init? You know, really listens to what you say. They don't carry on with what they're doing, nod their head and ignore you or change the subject. They look you in the eyes and want to know about your problems, problems that no one wants to hear or do anything about. I mean, Dad, don't listen, that's for sure. Too busy spending the little time he has with his new girlfriend and the new baby, the rest of it at work. Since she's had that kid, I might as well not exist, that's for sure.

Front of the takeaway.

Allan: Alright love, same again?

Liz: Er, yeah, can you wrap 'em up well, I don't want them to go cold on the way home.

Allan: Sure, it's freezing out there init love? Must be the weather that's keeping customers away. Do you have far to walk then?

Liz: Far enough in this rotten rain but what do you care?

159

Allan: Should have a coat on, you'll catch ya death. Does your mother know you're out like that?

Liz: Why would she bother? I could be out in a bikini and she wouldn't notice.

Allan: Ah, busy, is she?

Liz: She… being my, dad's girlfriend. Yeah, busy alright, with her new kid stuck to her chest… all day and all night.

Allan: Ah well love, we've all got to feed haven't we, even babies. Are you taking anything back for them?

Liz: No, they're just for me.

Allan: You could take her some of these I made earlier, I'm putting some new ones in the fryer now. She can have these for free, or your Dad can have them.

Liz: He won't be needing them… he'll be at work, paying for her and… his new baby.

Allan: All those extra mouths to feed, well someone's got to put food on the table.

Liz: Well, it certainly won't be her, she won't do any cooking or owt else for that matter. She never does a thing.

Allan: You don't sound very happy, do you?

Liz: I'm not.

Allan: You'll be fine when you've got your feet up watching TV, with ya fries.

160

Liz: You must be kidding, watching TV? I never get a chance to watch anything that I want. She's got the remote control glued on one hand… and her phone in the other. I don't even know how she holds that, kid!

Allan: Sounds like my old man, he never lets go of it and if he does for one second… my younger sister, Jada, grabs it and then… it's all-out war. She's about your age… always got something to say! I'm just glad, I don't live at home anymore… Your Stepmom sounds, err… busy… You err… can watch TV here for a bit if you want. I'll not disturb you; I'll be out front here sorting this lot out. It's gonna get busier soon. You can eat your food in peace.

Liz: Er, yeah right, who ya kidding? Why would I do that?

Allan: Hey, steady on, I'm only trying to help love. I've got the full, Sky package, watch anything you want. Your call… no problem either way…

Liz: I'm not sure. *(She stands, pauses and weighs up the situation.)*

Allan: It's a lot warmer in here than out there.

Liz: *(Direct address.)* I stood there in silence, looked outside, so why not? And in I went… to sit in his backroom… in peace. To watch TV and get fed for free, why not? It was great, I wasn't even missed by her. After that, I could go anytime I liked. I could get out of the house anytime I wanted and didn't have to listen to that racket of a screaming kid. If I was ever asked, 'Where ya been?' I just said, 'A friend's house from school.' In fact, the only thing I didn't like, was the thought of going home. It was boring. My Dad never in, or my Stepmom ignoring me. Allan never bored me, he always paid attention to me. He even bought me things.

Two weeks later in the back room of the takeaway, Liz has her feet up on the coffee table, watching TV and playing with her phone.

161

Allan: How you doing back here? See you making yourself at home.

Liz: Yeah, it's great, Allan, I just love watching TV on my own, no one turning it over without asking and then having to watch a load of rubbish. I tell ya, I'm so glad to be out of that house I could scream.

Allan: Not too loud I hope, but as I said earlier don't go spreading it to everyone.

Liz: You know I won't.

Allan: Right ok, but you know if you did, we'd both get into trouble. You with your dad and school, and me with my dad, you know what people are like?

Liz: No one knows, alright. I like coming here, so why would I want to lose this?

Allan: Yeah, ok. (*Changing tack.*) Hey, look what I've got you anyway, thought you could do with a new phone. Well not exactly a new one, it's my old one. But it's still better than that battered thing you've got. I've cleared it and put a new SIM in for you.

Liz: Oh thanks, Allan, that's brilliant.

Allan: I've put my number into it for you, ya can contact me anytime... but keep it to yourself mind.

Liz: (*Direct address.*) And I did keep it to myself, I never let anyone see it. It even had credit on it! I could search the internet, make as many calls as I like, well, not that many, 'cause I didn't have many people to ring. But the screen was so big, it was like having an iPad in my hand. And, of course, I could message people and people could message me practically for free.

162

Three weeks later at the back of the Take-Away.

Liz: What did you message me for?

Allan: I didn't want to ring you, because I've got you a surprise.

Liz: Yeah… What is it?

Allan: Sit down, close your eyes and I'll tell you.

Liz: OK, go on.

Allan: Right, open your eyes, this is for you. *(He unfolds a dress to her.)*

Liz: Oh, It's beautiful, I love it.

Allan: I thought you'd like it. It cost a bit but you're worth it. Try it on.

Liz: But.

Allan: Oh yeah, sure. I'll stand outside. *(He goes out, as she tries it on. It is short.)* Wow, it fits you so well. You look great.

Liz: *(Unsure.)* Do you think so?

Allan: Yeah… too right love, you look amazing… but, er… I think it's better if you just wear it in here, people might think

you've won the lottery if they see you in that. They might start asking questions.

Liz: Aye, even my, step-mum would ask questions on this… probably want to borrow it or have it herself.

Allan: So, you really like it?

163

Liz: Oh yeah, it's brilliant.

Allan: Good… and you still like coming here?

Liz: Yeah, I really do, the food, TV, phone and now… the dress. Thanks, Allan.

Allan: It's my pleasure … Come on, let's celebrate. *(He brings out two glasses and some bottles of cheap alcopops. He opens and pours them.)* Cheers.

Liz: *(Uncertain but reluctantly she joins in.)* Cheers. *(They both sit down on the couch.)* Aren't you bothered about the front of house, what if you have customers?

Allan: Always quiet on a Wednesday, locked up early. Cheers. *(They both drink and giggle.)* Tastes alright dun it?

Liz: Yeah, I once tasted my, Dad's beer and it was horrible… But this just tastes like… orange juice?

Allan: That's the good thing about it, it'll top you up with vitamin C, so you'll never catch a cold this winter! *(Allan chinks his glasses once more.)* Cheers.

Liz: *(Direct address.)* We carried on laughing and drinking into the early evening. I knew he was older than me by quite a few years, but he doesn't treat me like a child, we're just like best friends really, except we never fall out like. He would always ask about my friends, and school and why teachers were such a pain. Most of all, why my step-mum is a lazy cow and my dad is working all hours to look after her. I could tell Allan anything and… I did. He continued to listen to me and give me advice, which was, well, private between the two of us. Going to Allan's straight from school was the best, it gave us more time together and he would open the shop up later. He loved to surprise me, always buying me gifts, usually more clothes that I could wear at his place.

164

Allan: Hey listen, Liz, I'm gonna have to spend a bit more time in the front of the shop you know. I'm losing a lot of money and custom these last four weeks.

Liz: But I like it back here with just me and you together, watching TV and… you know, the other things.

Allan: Same… but I need to earn a living you know and get out front. I can't just sit back here and watch TV. Anyway, get that off, I'm talking, *(She turns the TV off.)* And all that food you're putting away, it has to be paid for somehow.

Liz: But I thought you liked cooking for me?

Alan: All these dresses and phones don't come for nowt you know.

Liz: What can I do, what can I do to help ya?

Allan: Well, if you must know… my brother's in a right state. His girlfriend left him, he's practically suicidal.

Liz: What's that got to do with me?

Allan: He just needs some company that's all. Someone who'll listen to him, like you do to me, you know, someone to share things with… like you do with me.

Liz: *(Shocked.)* But I thought, what I share with you is just between me and you. You said it were special between us and not to tell anyone?

Allan: That's right… apart from my, brother, that is. That's because I know he'd keep it quiet. I mean, what would your friends think… or your family, if they found out you've been eating all

165

this free food and drinking booze, lying about where you are? Imagine if they found out on Facebook or summat like that? They'd think all the bad things about you… and you're not like that are you… are you?

Liz: No, no I'm not.

Allan: So, I'll ask him to come round in an hour, alright?

Liz: Er… yeah… I suppose.

Allan: Good, I'll text him now.

Liz: *(Direct address.)* He'd bought me makeup and a new outfit all zipped up in a suede bag and asked me to get changed. I did and when I came out of the bathroom, I stumbled with the strap on my new shoes. Drinks were open on the coffee table, cans of cider. I sat down on the couch… then the door opened … with two men… standing there behind me. *(She turns to Allan.)* Who are these?

Allan: Friends of mine love, friends that I want you to take care of.

Liz: Eh, but what happened to your suicidal brother?

Allan: They all are, love. Think of yourself as a therapist, help talk 'em down from a great height… I bet you've got the gift for it.

Liz: But I don't want that gift.

Allan: What did you expect, all those presents didn't come for free… love?

~

Jada's Monologue *(Allan's younger sister)*

Jada is facing Allan who is now on remand behind prison bars.

Dad won't come, he's too hurt… he's heartbroken. He said, he feels ashamed of you. He feels ashamed of himself for not figuring this out… and then, for other people to point this out to him. He thinks people blame him, and that it's his fault… but it's not, is it? People are talking about stricter punishments for you shaming our family, I'm sure you know that… and you're going to court next week. Yesterday, a lady from a newspaper came to the house, they want to write things about you. How could you do it, what were you thinking? I mean, how you could look at her and do that, she's practically the same age as me, the same age as your own sister! What if someone did those things to me, how would you feel? Do you know how that makes me feel? People in school are blaming me… for what you've done. They stare at me on the bus, in lessons. I know what they're thinking… They don't say anything to my face but behind my back. Well? I've done nothing wrong. Maybe it's down to a lack of education, tarring us all with the same brush. Mum says I should hold my head up, we're good decent people, good neighbours… And we are… and you've… let us all down.

~

Tasks

Speaking and listening

'Free Gifts' is a play about gang grooming. It looks at how a lack of parental involvement left Liz open to abuse. **Task 1:** In pairs, without stereotyping, discuss what you think grooming is. Where can it happen? What are the different types of grooming? Who are the victims? Why are they singled out? Why do they let it happen? Who would you turn to for help? **Task 2:** Create a presentation that would make your peers more aware of grooming. Present it to the class.

Reading

On closer reading A Double Life. **Task 1:** Creating a worksheet, split up the features of how Liz is at home and how she is with Allan. What clues are there that she is at risk of becoming a victim of grooming?

Writing

Imagine you are the police officer who has arrested Allan. **Task 1:** Write the police officer's report up to the point of when Liz met Allan. Explain the reasons she got involved with him. Use statements from dad and Liz's step-mum that you think relevant to the report.

Extension Task: Fake people can also be described as phoney or false. They are in our society and can be manipulative for many reasons. Research how to spot people with fake motives. Think about fake texts/emails asking for your personal details. Why do they do this? Research.

https://www.youtube.com/watch?v=06SVzqzAdyw

18. Mobile Distractions

This is an introduction to basic Brecht in the style of an episodic play. It involves, multi-rolling by the cast of four, direct address on the delivery of lines and the opportunity for the cast to put the scenes in a non-linear order. Additionally, the play uses contrapuntal music (music opposite to the message in the scene that adds more meaning and raises questions) plus placards that narrate the message of the play as a piece of 'Theatre in Education.'

Characters
Mum/Dad
Child
Teen 1
Teen 2
Paramedic 1
Paramedic 2

Characters' names can be switched on gender. Take your pick, just remember to change the pronouns.

Mobile Safety Rap *All of the Actors*

Mobile safety - who needs you?
Crossing the road - is what we do.
Likes and selfies - cell phones, tablets.
Texting, swiping – it's all exciting.
No visual perception - cognitive connection.
Music, YouTube - safety disconnection.
On the road we walk - on the road we talk.
Slam on ya brakes - is it may be too late?

Scene 1: *The characters sit down centre stage, one in front, one behind the other to create a car.*

Mum: *(Direct address.)* If you only knew what it's like being the parent of a child that doesn't listen? 'For the last time, can you put your seatbelt on?'

Child: *(Direct address.)* And if you only knew what it's like for me, nag, nag, constant nag. 'Can you give me a minute, my coat is stuck in the belt?'

Mum: We're late as it is, hurry up. Have you got your bag?

Child: Yes.

Mum: Have you got your PE kit?

Child: Yes.

Mum: Everything?

Child: Yesss.

Mum: Right, let's go... at last!

Child: Hold on... I think I've left my homework on the table.

Mum: You what?

Child: Let me just check my bag, no, It's ok, I've picked it up. I'm ready, let's go... or I'll be late.

Mum: Don't push it. *(Pause, whilst mum drives the car.)*

Child: Can you change the channel, I hate this.

Mum: No... I'm listening for the traffic bulletins. I need to know if the bypass is still closed.

Child: *(On the iPhone.)* I'm gonna play my music then.

Mum: Put your earphones in.

Child: They're on the bed.

170

Mum: Well, don't play that too loud in here, it's distracting.

Child: That's not fair, why not? You shouldn't be putting lip gloss on whilst you're driving, that's distracting.

Mum: If I wasn't chasing you around the house to get ready and have breakfast, I'd have done it before I got in the car.

Child: Oh nooo, I've just realised. I've forgotten the money for the history trip, it needs to be handed in today. Er, sorry, mum, can you give me the money?

Mum: I wish you'd reminded me earlier, let me just check my purse, it's in my bag, I think I left it by the side of you. Pass it over.

Child: Yes, mum, it's here. *(Starts to pass it over the seat.)* Mum... look out!

At this point, the didactic messages written on placards before the performance are held up. What's written on them is spoken clearly in a direct address to the audience. This can be delivered by any of the actors in the group. Below are two examples:

Placard 1 '25% of global traffic accidents involve pedestrian casualties.'

Placard 2 'Not concentrating is the most frequent cause of road accidents?'

Scene 2: *Teen 1 is texting Teen 2 positioned on either side of the stage.*

Teen 1: *(Direct address.)* And one thing about teens, ten minutes is never ten minutes. *(Text noise sound.)* 'How long U gonna b!'

Teen 2: *(Direct address.)* When you're a teen, you've got your whole life ahead of you, so why rush? 'B with U in 10'... or thereabouts.

171

Teen 1: Brill, 'urry up n I can show u the new game I've bought before reg.

Teen 2: Going fast as.

Teen 1: Where r u now?

Teen 2: Cutting across Royd's Junction. Did u get that YouTube link I sent u?

Teen 1: Ye, awesome band, are u listening to it?

Teen 2: All morning.

Teen 1: Gonna get a cap like that… it's sick.

Teen 2: Dope man... (*Teen 2 stops texting and rings Teen 1, ringing noise sounds.*) Hey, have you found out who's on the team for tomorrow's match... should be on the notice board?

Teen 1: Do I sound like your personal slave?

Teen 2: No... Just the person who makes up for your terrible goalkeeping, and yes… I'm the one who scores all the goals and keeps us in the game.

Teen 1: I'm 4ever in your debt… Not!

Teen 2: So, have you checked?

Teen 1: Yep.

Teen 2: And?

Teen 1: Big surprise!

Teen 2: Get on with it.

Teen 1: I've took a pic of the team sheet; I'll ping it you.

Teen 2: Oh, you're too kind, I'm in suspense. (*Walks out across an imaginary road.*)

Teen 1: That's what friends are for. You should be receiving it… just about… now.

Placard 1 'Lst Txt?'

Placard 2 'iPhone/ dead Phone?'

Scene 3: *In the car.*

Child: Mum… look out!

Mum: Oh my goodness… I didn't see him.

Child: He just stepped out into the road, mum, he wasn't looking.

Both get out of the car to attend to the teen who is unconscious on the road.

Child: What you going to do, mum?

Mum: (*Badly shaken but quickly comes to her senses. She turns the imaginary car engine off and ushers the child back into the car.*) I want you to ring the emergency services. I know you've practised this in school. You need the paramedics. Explain what's happened and what I'm doing. We are at Royd's Junction, now… I'm going to treat him, he's not moving, tell them to hurry up.

Child: Yes, mum.

Mum: Pass me my jacket, please? (*The child does so at once whilst still on the phone. The mother carefully checks the child is in the recovery position and breathing. She takes her cardigan off, and places it on him to keep him warm.*)

Child: Er… Can I have the emergency services, please? We need paramedics to the scene of a road accident… yes, it's a teenager… I think. He's been hit by our car. We are at Royds Junction, Middletown… He's on the road, my mother is looking after him… The paramedics are on their way? Thank you… Yes, yes, I'll stay on the line, I'll tell mum.

Placard 1 'How do you make contact with emergency services, what is the procedure?'

Placard 2 'What is basic first aid?

Scene 4: *The Car (Centre stage, Teen1 multi-roles and becomes Paramedic 1, and Child becomes Paramedic 2. The changing of their roles is introduced directly to the audience.)*

Paramedic 1: *(Direct address.)* You may notice, I'm not a teen anymore. I'm now, a 30-year-old, Paramedic (*Turning to Teen 2 on the floor and tends to him.*) It's ok, can you hear me?

Paramedic 2: *(Direct address.)* And I've just grown from a young child to become a highly qualified assistant Paramedic, I'm also learning very fast. (*To the Teen.*) We're here to help you.

Teen 2: *(Starts to come around.)* What… where..?

Paramedic 2: We have movement.

Paramedic 1: Can you tell me exactly what happened? *(To the Mum.)*

174

Mum: I was driving my car and he walked out in front of me, I was momentarily distracted, but he was also distracted… he was on his phone.

Paramedic 1: Did you knock him in the air?

Mum: Yes.

Paramedic 2: That's an affirmative. *(Attending to the teenager.)*

Paramedic 1: *(Teen 2 starts to come around.)* Ok, keep relaxed, I'm just going to clear your airways and give you some oxygen.

Teen 2: Wait… What… Where's my phone?

Mum: It's here.

Paramedic 2: Don't worry about that, we have it here.

Paramedic 1: Who put him in this position?

Mum: I did.

Paramedic 1: Good job, you could have just saved his life.

Mum: As well as nearly taking it.

Paramedic 2: It usually takes two mistakes to create an accident.

Paramedic 1: Yes, both parties were not paying attention.

Paramedic 2: Ok, keep still. We are going to check your legs and your back.

Teen 2: *(Starts to move both slowly.)* I think I'm ok.

Paramedic 1: You know… *(Still checking Teen 2.)* I think you are.

175

Paramedic 2: You're very lucky,

Mum: Thank goodness. I'm one very… relieved driver.

Paramedic 1: You're coming around nicely but to be on the safe side, we're going to take you with us to the hospital, for a full check-up. *(They start to put the teen onto a stretcher.)*

Teen 2: *(Wearily.)* Will you do me a favour?

Paramedic 2: Sure, what is it?

Teen 2: Can you ring my school… ask them to take me off tomorrow's team sheet?

Placard 1 'What are dangerous distractions for pedestrians and motorists?'

Placard 2 'What can I learn from this?'

~

Teen 2's Monologue

Teen 2 is holding a new mobile phone. Characters' names can be switched on gender. Take your pick, just remember to change the pronouns.

I couldn't live without my mobile phone, who could? That's why I've got this model, because this Phone's got everything, and I mean everything! But here's a question, have you ever been walking somewhere and been looking down at your phone screen for so long, that you've completely lost track of time? You know, this morning, I said goodbye to my mum, closed the front door behind me, shut the garden gate and headed past the busy morning traffic… and still I can't recall any of it! That's what it's like when you're into something, whether playing a game, watching a video, picking your favourite song, friending someone on social media, googling your favourite team and who they're playing next? Like I said, this phone's got everything, I mean everything. Except… a brain, eyes and ears. That's what I've got, but… I wasn't thinking, I was talking about the game on Saturday. I was looking at the team sheet on my screen and listening to music, my favourite song… and then I stepped off the pavement, onto the road… and I nearly, oh so nearly, didn't hear that song ever again. So, yeah, I couldn't live without my mobile phone… but I nearly couldn't live with it.

~

Tasks

Speaking and listening

Bertolt Brecht is an important theatrical practitioner who made changes in the way audiences understood performances. Rather than being emotionally attached to the actors and themes of the play, Brecht wanted the audience to question the action and motives of the performers, also to question the message behind the play.

Discuss, in pairs and then as a group, what you think the play's main message is. **Task 1:** Research how Brecht's style of acting is different to a naturalistic style of acting. **Task 2:** Brecht's, style of theatre complements 'Theatre in Education.' This is where a message/learning experience is created for the audience to think about and question the play. Now, create your Brechtian play using similar conventions used in 'Mobile Distraction'. Create a list of five issues that affect teenagers. Pick your favourite and then script or devise a Brechtian performance, incorporating your own message to the class.

Reading

Drawing on your knowledge of reading plays, consider. **Task 1:** How does this style of writing differ from a traditional naturalistic play? How does the play inform the audience of the issues around the distractions of mobile phones? What impact would rearranging the scenes into a different time order make to an audience, in comparison to a linear structure?

Writing

Texting has created a variety of new vocabulary connected with mobile phones and their use. **Task 1:** Make a list of phrases and their acronyms (e.g., lol) to create a new dictionary of definitions and their meaning. **Task 2:** Write an article for your school magazine on the benefits and disadvantages of this new dictionary.

178

Extension Task: The play is written in an episodic style with the intentions of making an audience directly conscious and aware of the fact they are watching and questioning the underlying message of the play. In this particular play, its message is about how people ignore road safety when using mobile devices. This style of acting and performance was first introduced by Bertolt Brecht. Go to the link below and complete the tasks.

Research:
https://www.bbc.co.uk/bitesize/guides/zwmvd2p/revisio
n/1

19. Cross Country

Characters' names can be switched on gender. Take your pick, just remember to change the pronouns.

Characters
Georgia/George Bateman Teenage girl/boy

Sarah/Sam Childs - Teenage girl/boy

Beth/Ben Johnson - Teenage girl/boy

Mrs./Mr Shaw - Teacher

Scene: Running around the school playing field during cross-country, Beth stops behind a tree out of sight of Mrs Shaw, who is standing at the other end of the field. Beth ushers Sarah and Georgia over.

Mrs Shaw: Five laps left, six for you slow coaches at the back.

Beth: Why are we doing this?

Georgia: Doing what?

Beth: This nonsense, running around here like mice in a wheel. Yes, Miss, no, Miss, three bags full, Miss.

Sarah: What are you on about, Beth?

Beth: Rules, Sarah, rules. See Mrs Shaw over there? Do you see her running?

Georgia: No, but that's our teacher. They tell us what to do and we do it.

Sarah: That's how things work at school, Beth. Obviously, you haven't been paying attention.

180

Beth: You think, Mrs Shaw, could run around here? Must be at least sixty.

Mrs Shaw: Hey, you girls! Get out from behind that tree. What do you think this is, a mother's meeting? Beth Johnson, did you just shake your head at me? Two more laps for each of you.

Georgia: Oh, nice one, Beth, look what you've done now.

Sarah: No, Beth's right. I'm not doing those extra laps.

Beth: I'm not doing any.

Georgia: C'mon, Beth, we'll all be in big trouble if we don't get going now.

Beth: I'm not going anywhere. *(She checks her watch.)* I've done over 2000 steps already.

Sarah: What are you doing?

Beth: Sitting down on the grass, care to join me?

Sarah: You must be ma....

Mrs Shaw: Move it, now!

Beth: Sit down, Sarah! And you. Georgia.

Georgia: Please, Beth, just do the laps or we all will suffer.

Mrs Shaw: Right, that's it. Get here now, you stupid girls! *(Mrs Shaw jogs over to the group who are sitting down except for Georgia.)* You think you're the boss, sitting down when I called you over? You think you're in charge of this class? Unless you've forgotten, I'm the teacher. You listen to me. Rules. Order. Harmony.

Georgia: You've done it now, Beth.

Beth: What gives you your sense of authority… Miss?

Mrs Shaw: I beg your pardon! Detention for you, Beth Johnson. The rest of you will keep your traps shut if you know what's best for you.

Sarah: Can't you answer the question, Miss?

Mrs Shaw: Sarah Childs, you've just earned everyone a week's after school detention.

Georgia: Please, Miss, I've not said a word. My parents will go spare.

Mrs Shaw: Silence, girl!

Beth: The answer to the question you were unable to answer, Miss, is that we the students gave you the right to teach on our behalf. And now we're taking it back.

Mrs Shaw: I've a good mind to drag you by your laces, all the way to the Head's office!

Sarah: After intimidation, the threat of force. Rules. Order. Harmony. We're staying here on the floor.

Georgia: C'mon guys, the joke's over. Let's finish these laps like we were told.

Mrs Shaw: At last, the voice of reason. You really think you *allow* me to teach you? Don't make me laugh. I'm in control here, girls, be under no illusions about that.

Georgia: Yes, Miss.

Beth: We respectfully disagree, Miss. We're not moving.

Sarah: Consider it, a non-violent protest.

Mrs Shaw: You understand that being a student in this school requires you to abide by the rules?

Georgia: Yes, Miss. Absolutely, Miss.

Beth: But if we don't make clear which rules we find unjust, the teachers will never know. We're not moving until we speak to the Head.

Sarah: Beth…

Mrs Shaw: So be it. Georgia, get the head here immediately.

Georgia: Anything you ask, Miss.

Sarah: In this school, no one cares about the individual. Keep your head down, toe the line. That's the only way you make it out of here.

Mrs Shaw: You girls think you're special? Rules are for the common good, the end justifies the means. If some of you bad eggs get squeezed out of the side, then so be it.

Beth: We're not farm produce, Miss, we're people. If we want to run, we'll run. We don't need you telling us what to do.

Sarah: We're like slaves to the school.

Beth: There're more students than teachers in this school. We should decide the rules!

Mrs Shaw: You girls have a lot to learn about how the world works. The Head will be sure to fill you in on the fine print.

183

Georgia: I'm back, Miss.

Mrs Shaw: I can see that, Georgia, but one thing I cannot see is the Head! Can you not follow simple instructions?

Georgia: Miss, he said he was too busy for childish games. He gave me these two buckets and said you'd know what to do with them. I'm not going to be in any trouble, am I, Miss?

Mrs Shaw: Not if you keep watch over these two for a minute. I have a surprise in store for our young rebels. *(Mrs Shaw walks off around the corner.)*

Sarah: Georgia! What are you playing at? We should have stuck together, now look what's happened, she's split us up.

Beth: She wasn't cut out for it anyway Sarah, probably wants to be, Head Girl, sitting on the Head's shoulder like a parrot. Pretending to be a student when, really, she's the teachers' lapdog.

Georgia: I don't care what you guys think. You can't change a thing, so why are you even trying? If I play by the rules I can get by, you two will probably be expelled. For what, some meaningless protest?

Mrs Shaw: Everything alright over there, Georgia?

Georgia: Yes, Miss, everything's under control.

Sarah: Georgia, think beyond yourself for once. You enjoy running, so it's no problem for you to run fifteen times around this field. But for us it's pointless.

Beth: Who really benefits, or loses out, from me running around here? Only me! So, it should be my choice whether I run or not!

Georgia: We can't have a rule for everyone. Rule---

184

Sarah: Order!

Beth: Harmony! Yes, we get it!

Mrs Shaw: Right then girls, it's time for my favourite part-admission of wrongdoing!

Sarah: We haven't done anything wrong, our decision not to run didn't hurt you.

Mrs Shaw: Ahh the 'I know best' student syndrome. An apology, girls, and we can see that you only do two weeks' after school detentions for wasting my time.

Georgia: Very lenient, Miss.

Beth: I'm deeply remorseful… that you are unable to see the problems with this school system.

Mrs Shaw: Something funny, Childs?

Sarah: It's funny that we can't make our own choices, Miss.

Georgia: You couldn't be trusted to.

Mrs Shaw: Quite right, Georgia, I hope you're thirsty after your run, girls, because this water is ice cold. Georgia, this bucket is for you, let them have it!

Georgia throws a bucket of water over Beth. Mrs Shaw throws her bucket over Sarah.

~

Georgia's Monologue

Characters' names can be switched on gender. Take your pick, just remember to change the pronouns.

The 'Halloween Crazy Disco Party' I can't wait for it to start. It's in the gym after school today and it will be such a laugh. I've got my costume, it's brilliant. Everyone in our year is going, well, nearly everyone… apart from Beth and Sarah. They've still got their detentions to complete, with another four to go before they're done, and for what? I mean, my mum and dad have always encouraged me to stand up for what I believe in… but for something meaningless, that is just asking for trouble. Imagine turning up for a science lesson, refusing to do the task and then say I only like doing English lessons? I think, Beth's like that, she's always pushing things as far as she can… and if Sarah's stupid enough to follow her… well, that's her lookout. In fact, she told me she regrets it now but not to tell anyone. They must have written a book between them on school expectations, and I, for one, will not be losing any sleep over it. Anyway, I need as much energy as I can get, one lesson to go and the party is about to start… Yaaaa!!!

~

Tasks

Speaking and listening

Expressing opinions: In pairs, choose two characters from the play who describe Beth. **Task 1:** Make up and write down comments these characters might say about Beth that reflect their opinions and also their style of speaking. This can be developed further by experimenting with regional accents. **Task 2:** Act out an improvisation between the two characters, discussing the consequences of the protest and the detention.

Reading

At the beginning of the play, the students are running around the school playing field, before the protest develops. **Task 1:** Make notes about how this play could be performed on a stage in comparison to a film. Pick key moments from the play to highlight how could this be done effectively in both mediums. **Task 2:** Research the various types of theatre stages and auditoriums (audience positioning) used in drama. **Task 3:** Draw a plan of a stage, adding and incorporating audience, entrance and exit positions within the plan. Consider how you would stage 'Cross Country' and how effectively you could position the actors, so they are facing the audience. What props, lighting effects and sound effects would you use to enhance the performance?

Writing

In school, there are lots of rules we must follow - some given by law, some by the government, some created in school, but they're all there for a reason. What might the reasons be for the following rules: (1) having to wear a uniform (2) having to study given subjects (3) having to take a break from study in the morning or at lunchtimes. **Task 1:** Pick one of the above and justify the reasons for the rules in a letter to Sarah or Beth.

Extension Task: Rules are a very important part of school life, as well as life in general. Self-control is a predictor of development and success in your personal, social, school and work life. Could this help you?

Research
https://www.youtube.com/watch?v=XxEDFPzNUYQ

20. The Wall

Characters
Mr Ellis, Head of Year
Mrs Darshon, Zaine's mother.

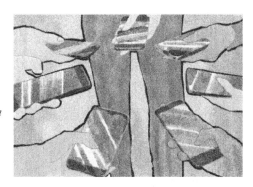

Characters' names can be switched on gender. Take your pick, just remember to change the pronouns.

Scene: *The Head of Year's Office.*

Mr Ellis: Good morning, Mrs Darshon, please take a seat.

Mrs Darshon: Yes, of course, thank you for seeing me at such short notice, Mr Ellis. I appreciate it.

Mr Ellis: Not a problem, so how can I help you?

Mrs Darshon: It's about my son, Zaine. I'm worried about him.

Mr Ellis: Really, why is that?

Mrs Darshon: Well, he just seems different lately, he… doesn't want to come to school.

Mr Ellis: Yes, I have his attendance record here in front of me, there has been a dip of late over the last six weeks. However, every absence has been rung in by yourself or, Mr Darshon, there has been no truanting to my knowledge. Am I correct?

Mrs Darshon: Yes, he's had a stomach bug, it's been quite prolonged.

Mr Ellis: Have you been to the doctors with, Zaine, about it?

Mrs Darshon: Yes, er… she gave him some medicine. I er… don't think it's working because he didn't feel well enough to come to school today.

Mr Ellis: But he was in yesterday I see *(Looking at a screen.)* and parts of last week.

Mrs Darshon: Yes. I know, but he seems to get bad stomach cramps, they just seem to come out of the blue… when he's getting ready for school.

Mr Ellis: Do they ease off during the day?

Mrs Darshon: I guess so, but it's hard to tell, he just stays in his room, probably because he's ill, but it's hard to tell.

Mr Ellis: Does he come out of his room much?

Mrs Darshon: Not really, he prefers his own space… recently.

Mr Ellis: When you say recently, you mean within the last 6 weeks?

Mrs Darshon: That's right, Mr Ellis.

Mr Ellis: Have you tried to talk to him about his isolation, why, all of a sudden, he prefers to be alone?

Mrs Darshon: He doesn't want to talk much, I mean, last week he wouldn't answer me, even when I was standing outside his bedroom door.

Mr Ellis: Did he come out then?

Mrs Darshon: Well, er, not exactly, I went in… eventually.

190

Mr Ellis: Eventually?

Mrs Darshon: I er… forced my way in, well I'm really worried. I didn't want to… but I got so angry and then when I was in… he just stared at his phone screen whilst I tried to talk to him.

Mr Ellis: Did you ask him to put it down, whilst you tried to talk to him.

Mrs Darshon: Yes, I did, but here's the odd thing, when I asked him, he wouldn't respond. He was silent… for a long time. I asked him again and then he screamed at me… almost crying. We had a blazing row, I told him, 'Who do you think you are shouting at me like that?'… I er… told him to stay in his room… till he apologises.

Mr Ellis: Which is the one thing you didn't want… him staying in his bedroom.

Mrs Darshon: Yes, that's right… I know he's just become a teenager and they go through a lot of changes but it's…

Mr Ellis: Irrational?

Mrs Darshon: Yes, it is… very. How is he doing at school?

Mr Ellis: Exemplary, the last couple of years. Full attendance, excellent punctuality and a hard-working conscientious pupil. Just this small blip on attendance throughout his illness. Interestingly, I did hear from his English teacher, Mr Johnson, that he was given a detention for not completing his classwork on time. I remember it because, Mr Johnson said, 'Zaine, seemed to enjoy the detention.'

Mrs Darshon: Enjoy a detention?

Mr Ellis: Yes, apparently he even asked, Mr Johnson, if he could work in his classroom all lunchtime, to add more detail to his work and complete it. Mr Johnson also mentioned that Zaine seemed very tired, like he was lacking sleep or maybe still struggling with this stomach bug. Is there anything you have noticed about Zaine, Mrs Darshon, anything physical?

Mrs Darshon: Er… actually I've mentioned it to his father, he seems to be getting very thin. He eats less than a sparrow, my husband thinks it's down to this bug. That's still unusual isn't it, Mr Ellis?

Mr Ellis: Yes, I suppose so, and you think the bug could well be the cause of tiredness?

Mrs Darshon: I also don't think he's getting enough sleep.

Mr Ellis: Why, does he go to bed late?

Mrs Darshon: Not really, he's in bed early but his sleeping pattern seems disturbed. I keep telling him to turn his phone off or I'll confiscate it from him.

Mr Ellis: And did you?

Mrs Darshon: Er, Yes for a while… but we ended up having another big row, I tried to take it off him to have a look at what might be bothering him… but he went hysterical. He doesn't like anyone going near it, like I said he's always looking at it.

Mr Ellis: Teenagers and their phones, but it does seem odd that he's constantly looking at it all the time, I don't think that's a good thing. Is he still interested in gymnastics, Mrs Darshon? I hear he is very good at it. Exercise is the best thing for rest and a good night's sleep.

Mrs Darshon: No, he seems to have lost a lot of interest in any sports, maybe that's because of that fall he had on the trampoline, I think it's knocked his confidence for a while. That large graze under his eye is still there.

Mr Ellis: Falling off a trampoline and picking up a large graze under his eye? I would have heard of that. Ok, have you noticed any other psychological changes in, Zaine, for example when you try and speak to him about what he might be interested in, you know like films, sport, friends, that kind of thing?

Mrs Darshon: Speak to him… I can't speak to him. He won't respond to me, or his father. If I say, 'What's up with you?' It's a 'Nothing' or, 'Leave me alone.' Or if I say, 'Why don't you go out to kick a football with your mates?' He'll say, 'I hate football and I'm useless at it and my mates are busy.'

Mr Ellis: Has he mentioned any boys or girls who he doesn't like?

Mrs Darshon: He did mention some names, but I can't remember them, I mean, most teenagers fall in and fall out with friends. Just like adults do. I just can't get through to him.

Mr Ellis: Right, I think I have got a much better picture of what's going on with, Zaine. Clearly, he has a problem and this is putting him off coming into school. What we have to do is get to the root of the problem straight away.

Mrs Darshon: But what is it… and what can I do?

Mr Ellis: Ok, here's my advice…

~

Mrs Darshon's Monologue

Characters' names can be switched on gender. Take your pick, just remember to change the pronouns.

I realised I was going about it the wrong way with Zaine, after my last conversation with, Mr Ellis. I have to break this wall down between us, so I tried a different approach with him. I asked him, gently, if we could go for a walk together in the park... and we did. We walked for a long time, not really saying much. I bought him an ice cream and we sat on a park bench... I put my arm around him and told him... I was once bullied at school and what did he think about that? Then he put his head down... I thought he was going to block me... again... and then... he quietly explained that he always liked to put his hand up in class, especially when he knew the answers. It started in his French lesson. The teacher asked, what is 'Garcon?' When Zaine answered, a boy picked up on our family name and made a joke about it. Darshon - Garcon. Zaine said he just laughed it off but... it didn't stop there. Afterwards, other boys started to call him that and when they realised he didn't challenge them ... they thought it was acceptable. Some boys started to hit him if he didn't respond to that name, treating him like a young waiter... getting him to do jobs for them. He showed me his phone... constant threats online. He's even changed his name on social media to please them and stop them bullying him... but it hasn't... yet. But it will now. I rang Mr Ellis and he's furious and called the boy's parents into school tomorrow.

~

194

Tasks

Speaking and listening
Create a debate for a morning radio show on the issues of 'Bullying Today'. Write down a list of questions that a presenter might ask that would help lead someone to deal with bullying better in the future. **Task 1:** Split the stage into two areas, *(Split-screen)* one in the radio studio with the presenter and guests, the other where a flashback of the incidents take place. Try to focus on psychological bullying or cyberbullying from imaginary incidents, giving sound advice throughout the performance.

Reading
Looking closely at the play again, imagine you are, Mr Ellis. What clues are there on why the victim is being bullied and how? Why is the victim doing nothing about it? **Task 1:** What advice do you think Mr Ellis gave Mrs Darshon after the closing line, 'Ok, here's my advice? **Task 2:** Make three columns and compare notes with the person sat next to you.

Writing
Imagine, Mr Ellis fact-checking with the English teacher, Mr Johnson, and the PE teacher about Zaine's claim that he had a fall in the PE lesson. **Task 1:** As Zaine's Head of Year, imagine you are Mr Ellis writing a report of the discussion with Mrs Darshon. Support your thoughts with factual detail to come to a growing knowledge of what is happening to Zaine. Bring the report to a summative conclusion to keep as a record of the incidents.

Extension Task: Research cyberbullying and its impact on teenagers.
https://www.youtube.com/watch?v=hCcT1BaWGqk

Acknowledgements

Λ big thank you to my family, friends and colleagues. Your support has been invaluable. To all of my students who have helped 'fine tune' all the plays and activities in lessons and extra-curricular drama clubs, again many thanks for your input. And finally, to Diana Grebennikova for her creative and thoughtful illustrations, spasibo.

About the Author

A Bretton Hall trained, Theatre Arts graduate; Gary Baxendale is a drama teacher with over 20 years' secondary classroom experience and has been a drama examiner since 2005. He currently teaches in West Yorkshire.

www.garybaxendale.co.uk